<br>AF345485

**ADELINE VIRGINIA WOOLF** 25 January 1882 – 28 March 1941 was an English writer, considered one of the most important modernist 20th-century authors and a pioneer in the use of stream of consciousness as a narrative device.

# Virginia Woolf

# A HAUNTED HOUSE

## AND OTHER WRITINGS

DELHI OPEN BOOKS

**Published by**

**D⬚B**

**Delhi Open Books**

G/F, 4771/23, Bharat Ram Road, Daryaganj, New Delhi-110002
Ph.: 91-11-42408081
E-mail: **delhiopenbooks2016@gmail.com**

ISBN: 978-81-961623-0-6

Cover, Typesetting, and Book Design by **ROHIT**

# Contents

# A Haunted House

Whatever hour you woke there was a door shutting. From room to room they went, hand in hand, lifting here, opening there, making sure--a ghostly couple.

"Here we left it," she said. And he added, "Oh, but here tool" "It's upstairs," she murmured. "And in the garden," he whispered. "Quietly," they said, "or we shall wake them."

But it wasn't that you woke us. Oh, no. "They're looking for it; they're drawing the curtain," one might say, and so read on a page or two. "Now they've found it,' one would be certain, stopping the pencil on the margin. And then, tired of reading, one might rise and see for oneself, the house all empty, the doors standing open, only the wood pigeons bubbling with content and the hum of the threshing machine sounding from the farm. "What did I come in here for? What did I want to find?" My hands were empty. "Perhaps its upstairs then?" The apples were in the loft. And so down again, the garden still as ever, only the book had slipped into the grass.

But they had found it in the drawing room. Not that one could ever see them. The windowpanes reflected apples, reflected roses; all the leaves were green in the glass. If they moved in the drawing room, the apple only turned its yellow side. Yet, the moment after, if the door was opened, spread about the floor, hung upon the walls, pendant from the ceiling--what? My hands were empty. The shadow of a thrush crossed the carpet; from the deepest wells of silence the wood pigeon drew its bubble of sound. "Safe, safe, safe" the pulse of the house beat softly. "The treasure buried; the room . . ." the pulse stopped short. Oh, was that the buried treasure?

A moment later the light had faded. Out in the garden

then? But the trees spun darkness for a wandering beam of sun. So fine, so rare, coolly sunk beneath the surface the beam I sought always burned behind the glass. Death was the glass; death was between us, coming to the woman first, hundreds of years ago, leaving the house, sealing all the windows; the rooms were darkened. He left it, left her, went North, went East, saw the stars turned in the Southern sky; sought the house, found it dropped beneath the Downs. "Safe, safe, safe," the pulse of the house beat gladly. 'The Treasure yours."

The wind roars up the avenue. Trees stoop and bend this way and that. Moonbeams splash and spill wildly in the rain. But the beam of the lamp falls straight from the window. The candle burns stiff and still. Wandering through the house, opening the windows, whispering not to wake us, the ghostly couple seek their joy.

"Here we slept," she says. And he adds, "Kisses without number." "Waking in the morning--" "Silver between the trees--" "Upstairs--" 'In the garden--" "When summer came--" 'In winter snowtime--" "The doors go shutting far in the distance, gently knocking like the pulse of a heart.

Nearer they come, cease at the doorway. The wind falls, the rain slides silver down the glass. Our eyes darken, we hear no steps beside us; we see no lady spread her ghostly cloak. His hands shield the lantern. "Look," he breathes. "Sound asleep. Love upon their lips."

Stooping, holding their silver lamp above us, long they look and deeply. Long they pause. The wind drives straightly; the flame stoops slightly. Wild beams of moonlight cross both floor and wall, and, meeting, stain the faces bent; the faces pondering; the faces that search the sleepers and seek their hidden joy.

"Safe, safe, safe," the heart of the house beats proudly. "Long years--" he sighs. "Again you found me." "Here," she murmurs, "sleeping; in the garden reading; laughing, rolling apples in the loft. Here we left our treasure--" Stooping, their light lifts the lids upon my eyes. "Safe! safe! safe!" the pulse of the house beats wildly. Waking, I cry "Oh, is this your buried treasure? The light in the heart."

# An Unwritten Novel

SUCH AN EXPRESSION of unhappiness was enough by itself to make one's eyes slide above the paper's edge to the poor woman's face, insignificant without that look, almost a symbol of human destiny with it. Life's what you see in people's eyes; life's what they learn, and, having learnt it, never, though they seek to hide it, cease to be aware of what? That life's like that, it seems. Five faces oppositefive mature faces and the knowledge in each face. Strange, though, how people want to conceal it! Marks of reticence are on all those faces: lips shut, eyes shaded, each one of the five doing something to hide or stultify his knowledge. One smokes; another reads; a third checks entries in a pocket book; a fourth stares at the map of the line framed opposite; and the fifth the terrible thing about the fifth is that she does nothing at all. She looks at life. Ah, but my poor, unfortunate woman, do play the game do, for all our sakes, conceal it!

As if she heard me, she looked up, shifted slightly in her seat and sighed. She seemed to apologise and at the same time to say to me, "If only you knew!" Then she looked at life again. "But I do know," I answered silently, glancing at the Times for manners' sake. "I know the whole business. 'Peace between Germany and the Allied Powers was yesterday officially ushered in at Paris Signor Nitti, the Italian Prime Ministera passenger train at Doncaster was in collision with a goods train...' We all know the Times knows but we pretend we don't." My eyes had once more crept over the paper's rim. She shuddered, twitched her arm queerly to the middle of her back and shook her head. Again I dipped into my great reservoir of life. "Take what you like," I continued, "births, death, marriages, Court Circular, the habits of birds, Leonardo da Vinci, the Sandhills murder, high wages and the cost of living, oh, take what you like," I repeated, "it's all in the Times!" Again with infinite weariness she moved her head from side to side until, like a top exhausted with spinning, it settled on her neck.

The Times was no protection against such sorrow as hers. But other human beings forbade intercourse. The best thing to do against life was to fold the paper so that it made a perfect square, crisp, thick, impervious even to life. This done, I glanced up quickly, armed with a shield of my own. She pierced through my shield; she gazed into my eyes as if searching any sediment of courage at the depths of them and damping it to clay. Her twitch alone denied all hope, discounted all illusion.

So we rattled through Surrey and across the border into Sussex. But with my eyes upon life I did not see that the other travellers had left, one by one, till, save for the man who read, we were alone together. Here was Three Bridges station. We drew slowly down the platform and stopped. Was he going to leave us? I prayed both waysI prayed last that he might stay. At that instant he roused himself, crumpled his paper contemptuously, like a thing done with, burst open the door, and left us alone.

The unhappy woman, leaning a little forward, palely and colourlessly addressed me talked of stations and holidays, of brothers at Eastbourne, and the time of the year, which was, I forget now, early or late. But at last looking from the window and seeing, I knew, only life, she breathed, "Staying away that's the drawback of it" Ah, now we approached the catastrophe, "My sister-in-law" the bitterness of her tone was like lemon on cold steel, and speaking, not to me, but to herself, she muttered, "nonsense, she would say that's what they all say," and while she spoke she fidgeted as though the skin on her back were as a plucked fowl's in a poulterer's shop-window.

"Oh, that cow!" she broke off nervously, as though the great wooden cow in the meadow had shocked her and saved her from some indiscretion. Then she shuddered, and then she made the awkward, angular movement that I had seen before, as if, after the spasm, some spot between the shoulders burnt or itched. Then again she looked the most unhappy woman in the world, and I once more reproached her, though not with the same conviction, for if there were a reason, and if I knew the reason, the stigma was removed from life.

"Sisters-in-law," I said

Her lips pursed as if to spit venom at the word; pursed they remained. All she did was to take her glove and rub hard at a spot on the window-pane. She rubbed as if she would rub something out for eversome stain, some indelible contamination. Indeed, the spot remained for all her rubbing, and back she sank with the shudder and the clutch of the arm I had come to expect. Something impelled me to take my glove and rub my window. There, too, was a little speck on the glass. For all my rubbing, it remained. And then the spasm went through me; I crooked my arm and plucked at the middle of my back. My skin, too, felt like the damp chicken's skin in the poulterer's shop-window; one spot between the shoulders itched and irritated, felt clammy, felt raw. Could I reach it? Surreptitiously I tried. She saw me. A smile of infinite irony, infinite sorrow, flitted and faded from her face. But she had communicated, shared her secret, passed her poison; she would speak no more. Leaning back in my corner, shielding my eyes from her eyes, seeing only the slopes and hollows, greys and purples, of the winter's landscape, I read her message, deciphered her secret, reading it beneath her gaze.

Hilda's the sister-in-law. Hilda? Hilda? Hilda Marsh Hilda the blooming, the full bosomed, the matronly. Hilda stands at the door as the cab draws up, holding a coin. "Poor Minnie, more of a grasshopper than ever old cloak she had last year. Well, well, with two children these days one can't do more. No, Minnie, I've got it; here you are, cabby none of your ways

                    A Haunted House and other writings

with me. Come in, Minnie. Oh, I could carry you, let alone your basket!" So they go into the dining-room. "Aunt Minnie, children."

Slowly the knives and forks sink from the upright. Down they get (Bob and Barbara), hold out hands stiffly; back again to their chairs, staring between the resumed mouthfuls. [But this we'll skip; ornaments, curtains, trefoil china plate, yellow oblongs of cheese, white squares of biscuits kip oh, but wait! Half-way through luncheon one of those shivers; Bob stares at her, spoon in mouth. "Get on with your pudding, Bob;" but Hilda disapproves. "Why should she twitch?" Skip, skip, till we reach the landing on the upper floor; stairs brass-bound; linoleum worn; oh, yes! little bedroom looking out over the roofs of Eastbourne zigzagging roofs like the spines of caterpillars, this way, that way, striped red and yellow, with blue-black slating]. Now, Minnie, the door's shut; Hilda heavily descends to the basement; you unstrap the straps of your basket, lay on the bed a meagre nightgown, stand side by side furred felt slippers. The looking-glass no, you avoid the looking-glass. Some methodical disposition of hat-pins. Perhaps the shell box has something in it? You shake it; it's the pearl stud there was last year that's all. And then the sniff, the sigh, the sitting by the window. Three o'clock on a December afternoon; the rain drizzling; one light low in the skylight of a drapery emporium; another high in a servant's bedroom this one goes out. That gives her nothing to look at. A moment's blankness then, what are you thinking? (Let me peep across at her opposite; she's asleep or pretending it; so what would she think about sitting at the window at three o'clock in the afternoon? Health, money, hills, her God?) Yes, sitting on the very edge of the chair looking over the roofs of Eastbourne, Minnie Marsh prays to God. That's all very well; and she may rub the pane too, as though to see God better; but what God does she see? Who's the God of Minnie Marsh, the God of the back streets of Eastbourne, the God of three o'clock in the afternoon? I, too, see roofs, I see sky; but, oh, dear this seeing of Gods! More like President Kruger than Prince Albert that's the best I can do for him; and I see him on a chair, in a black frock-coat, not so very high up either; I can manage a cloud or two for him to sit on; and then his hand trailing in the clouds holds a rod, a truncheon is it?black, thick, horned a brutal old bullyMinnie's God! Did he send the itch and the patch and the twitch? Is that why she prays? What she rubs on the window is the stain of sin. Oh, she committed some crime!

I have my choice of crimes. The woods flit and fly in summer there are bluebells; in the opening there, when Spring comes, primroses. A parting, was it, twenty years ago? Vows broken? Not Minnie's!...She was faithful. How she nursed her mother! All her savings on the tombstone wreaths under glass daffodils in jars. But I'm off the track. A crime...They would say she kept her sorrow, suppressed her secret her sex, they'd say the scientific people. But what flummery to saddle her with sex! Nomore like this. Passing down the streets of Croyden twenty years ago, the violet loops of ribbon in the draper's window spangled in the electric light catch her eye. She lingers past six. Still by running she can reach home. She pushes through the glass swing door. It's sale-time. Shallow trays brim with ribbons. She pauses, pulls this, fingers that with the raised roses on itno need to choose, no need to buy, and each tray with its surprises. "We don't shut till seven," and then it is seven. She runs, she rushes, home she reaches, but too late. Neighbours the doctor baby brother the kettles calded hospital dead or only the shock of it, the blame? Ah, but the detail matters nothing! It's what she carries with her; the spot, the crime, the thing to expiate, always there between her shoulders. "Yes," she seems to nod to me, "it's the thing I did."

Whether you did, or what you did, I don't mind; it's not the thing I want. The draper's window looped with violet that'll do; a little cheap perhaps, a little commonplace since one has a choice of crimes, but then so many (let me peep across again

                    A Haunted House and other writings

still sleeping, or pretending to sleep! white, worn, the mouth closed a touch of obstinacy, more than one would think no hint of sex) so many crimes aren't your crime; your crime was cheap; only the retribution solemn; for now the church door opens, the hard wooden pew receives her; on the brown tiles she kneels; every day, winter, summer, dusk, dawn (here she's at it) prays. All her sins fall, fall, for ever fall. The spot receives them. It's raised, it's red, it's burning. Next she twitches. Small boys point. "Bob at lunch to-day"But elderly women are the worst.

Indeed now you can't sit praying any longer. Kruger's sunk beneath the cloudswashed over as with a painter's brush of liquid grey, to which he adds a tinge of blackeven the tip of the truncheon gone now. That's what always happens! Just as you've seen him, felt him, someone interrupts. It's Hilda now.

How you hate her! She'll even lock the bathroom door overnight, too, though it's only cold water you want, and sometimes when the night's been bad it seems as if washing helped. And John at breakfast the children meals are worst, and sometimes there are friends ferns don't altogether hide 'em they guess, too; so out you go along the front, where the waves are grey, and the papers blow, and the glass shelters green and draughty, and the chairs cost tuppence too much for there must be preachers along the sands. Ah, that's a niggerthat's a funny man that's a man with parakeets poor little creatures! Is there no one here who thinks of God?just up there, over the pier, with his rod but no there's nothing but grey in the sky or if it's blue the white clouds hide him, and the music it's military musicand what are they fishing for? Do they catch them? How the children stare! Well, then home a back way"Home a back way!" The words have meaning; might have been spoken by the old man with whiskers no, no, he didn't really speak; but everything has meaning placards leaning against doorways names above shop-windows red fruit in baskets women's heads in the hairdresser's all say "Minnie Marsh!" But here's a jerk. "Eggs are cheaper!" That's what always happens! I was heading her over the waterfall, straight for madness, when, like a flock of dream sheep, she turns t'other way and runs between my fingers. Eggs are cheaper. Tethered to the shores of the world, none of the crimes, sorrows, rhapsodies, or insanities for poor Minnie Marsh; never late for luncheon; never caught in a storm without a mackintosh; never utterly unconscious of the cheapness of eggs. So she reaches home scrapes her boots.

Have I read you right? But the human face the human face at the top of the fullest sheet of print holds more, withholds more. Now, eyes open, she looks out; and in the human eye how d'you define it?there's a break a division so that when you've grasped the stem the butterfly's off the moth that hangs in the evening over the yellow flowermove, raise your hand, off, high, away. I won't raise my hand. Hang still, then, quiver, life, soul, spirit, whatever you are of Minnie MarshI, too, on my flowerthe hawk over the downalone, or what were the worth of life? To rise; hang still in the evening, in the midday; hang still over the down. The flicker of a handoff, up! then poised again. Alone, unseen; seeing all so still down there, all so lovely. None seeing, none caring. The eyes of others our prisons; their thoughts our cages. Air above, air below. And the moon and immortality...Oh, but I drop to the turf! Are you down too, you in the corner, what's your namewomanMinnie Marsh; some such name as that? There she is, tight to her blossom; opening her hand-bag, from which she takes a hollow shellan eggwho was saying that eggs were cheaper? You or I? Oh, it was you who said it on the way home, you remember, when the old gentleman, suddenly opening his umbrella or sneezing was it? Anyhow, Kruger went, and you came "home a back way," and scraped your boots. Yes. And now you lay across your knees a pocket-handkerchief into which drop little angular fragments of egg shell fragments of a map a puzzle. I wish I could piece them together! If you would only sit still. She's moved her knees the map's in bits again. Down the slopes of the

Andes the white blocks of marble go bounding and hurtling, crushing to death a whole troop of Spanish muleteers, with their convoyDrake's booty, gold and silver. But to return

To what, to where? She opened the door, and, putting her umbrella in the stand that goes without saying; so, too, the whiff of beef from the basement; dot, dot, dot. But what I cannot thus eliminate, what I must, head down, eyes shut, with the courage of a battalion and the blindness of a bull, charge and disperse are, indubitably, the figures behind the ferns, commercial travellers. There I've hidden them all this time in the hope that somehow they'd disappear, or better still emerge, as indeed they must, if the story's to go on gathering richness and rotundity, destiny and tragedy, as stories should, rolling along with it two, if not three, commercial travellers and a whole grove of aspidistra. "The fronds of the aspidistra only partly concealed the commercial traveller" Rhododendrons would conceal him utterly, and into the bargain give me my fling of red and white, for which I starve and strive; but rhododendrons in Eastbournein Decemberon the Marshes' tableno, no, I dare not; it's all a matter of crusts and cruets, frills and ferns. Perhaps there'll be a moment later by the sea. Moreover, I feel, pleasantly pricking through the green fretwork and over the glacis of cut glass, a desire to peer and peep at the man oppositeone's as much as I can manage. James Moggridge is it, whom the Marshes call Jimmy? [Minnie, you must promise not to twitch till I've got this straight]. James Moggridge travels inshall we say buttons?but the time's not come for bringing them inthe big and the little on the long cards, some peacock-eyed, others dull gold; cairngorms some, and others coral sprays but I say the time's not come. He travels, and on Thursdays, his Eastbourne day, takes his meals with the Marshes. His red face, his little steady eyes by no means altogether commonplace his enormous appetite (that's safe; he won't look at Minnie till the bread's swamped the gravy dry), napkin tucked diamond-wise but this is primitive, and whatever it may do the reader, don't take me in. Let's dodge to the Moggridge household, set that in motion. Well, the family boots are mended on Sundays by James himself. He reads *Truth*. But his passion? Roses and his wife a retired hospital nurse interesting for God's sake let me have one woman with a name I like! But no; she's of the unborn children of the mind, illicit, none the less loved, like my rhododendrons. How many die in every novel that's written the best, the dearest, while Moggridge lives. It's life's fault. Here's Minnie eating her egg at the moment opposite and at t'other end of the line are we past Lewes?there must be Jimmy or what's her twitch for?

There must be Moggridgelife's fault. Life imposes her laws; life blocks the way; life's behind the fern; life's the tyrant; oh, but not the bully! No, for I assure you I come willingly; I come wooed by Heaven knows what compulsion across ferns and cruets, tables splashed and bottles smeared. I come irresistibly to lodge myself somewhere on the firm flesh, in the robust spine, wherever I can penetrate or find foothold on the person, in the soul, of Moggridge the man. The enormous stability of the fabric; the spine tough as whalebone, straight as oak-tree; the ribs radiating branches; the flesh taut tarpaulin; the red hollows; the suck and regurgitation of the heart; while from above meat falls in brown cubes and beer gushes to be churned to blood again and so we reach the eyes. Behind the aspidistra they see something; black, white, dismal; now the plate again; behind the aspidistra they see elderly woman; "Marsh's sister, Hilda's more my sort;" the tablecloth now. "Marsh would know what's wrong with Morrises..." talk that over; cheese has come; the plate again; turn it round the enormous fingers; now the woman opposite. "Marsh's sister not a bit like Marsh; wretched, elderly female....You should feed your hens....God's truth, what's set her twitching? Not what I said? Dear, dear, dear! These elderly women. Dear, dear!"

[Yes, Minnie; I know you've twitched, but one momentJames Moggridge].

   

"Dear, dear, dear!" How beautiful the sound is! like the knock of a mallet on seasoned timber, like the throb of the heart of an ancient whaler when the seas press thick and the green is clouded. "Dear, dear!" what a passing bell for the souls of the fretful to soothe them and solace them, lap them in linen, saying, "So long. Good luck to you!" and then, "What's your pleasure?" for though Moggridge would pluck his rose for her, that's done, that's over. Now what's the next thing? "Madam, you'll miss your train," for they don't linger.

That's the man's way; that's the sound that reverberates; that's St. Paul's and the motor-omnibuses. But we're brushing the crumbs off. Oh, Moggridge, you won't stay? You must be off? Are you driving through Eastbourne this afternoon in one of those little carriages? Are you the man who's walled up in green cardboard boxes, and sometimes has the blinds down, and sometimes sits so solemn staring like a sphinx, and always there's a look of the sepulchral, something of the undertaker, the coffin, and the dusk about horse and driver? Do tell mebut the doors slammed. We shall never meet again. Moggridge, farewell!

Yes, yes, I'm coming. Right up to the top of the house. One moment I'll linger. How the mud goes round in the mindwhat a swirl these monsters leave, the waters rocking, the weeds waving and green here, black there, striking to the sand, till by degrees the atoms reassemble, the deposit sifts itself, and again through the eyes one sees clear and still, and there comes to the lips some prayer for the departed, some obsequy for the souls of those one nods to, the people one never meets again.

James Moggridge is dead now, gone for ever. Well, Minnie"I can face it no longer." If she said that(Let me look at her. She is brushing the eggshell into deep declivities). She said it certainly, leaning against the wall of the bedroom, and plucking at the little balls which edge the claret-coloured curtain. But when the self speaks to the self, who is speaking?the entombed soul, the spirit driven in, in, in to the central catacomb; the self that took the veil and left the worlda coward perhaps, yet somehow beautiful, as it flits with its lantern restlessly up and down the dark corridors. "I can bear it no longer," her spirit says. "That man at lunchHildathe children." Oh, heavens, her sob! It's the spirit wailing its destiny, the spirit driven hither, thither, lodging on the diminishing carpetsmeagre footholdsshrunken shreds of all the vanishing universelove, life, faith, husband, children, I know not what splendours and pageantries glimpsed in girlhood. "Not for menot for me."

But thenthe muffins, the bald elderly dog? Bead mats I should fancy and the consolation of underlinen. If Minnie Marsh were run over and taken to hospital, nurses and doctors themselves would exclaim....There's the vista and the visionthere's the distancethe blue blot at the end of the avenue, while, after all, the tea is rich, the muffin hot, and the dog"Benny, to your basket, sir, and see what mother's brought you!" So, taking the glove with the worn thumb, defying once more the encroaching demon of what's called going in holes, you renew the fortifications, threading the grey wool, running it in and out.

Running it in and out, across and over, spinning a web through which God himselfhush, don't think of God! How firm the stitches are! You must be proud of your darning. Let nothing disturb her. Let the light fall gently, and the clouds show an inner vest of the first green leaf. Let the sparrow perch on the twig and shake the raindrop hanging to the twig's elbow.... Why look up? Was it a sound, a thought? Oh, heavens! Back again to the thing you did, the plate glass with the violet loops? But Hilda will come. Ignominies, humiliations, oh! Close the breach.

Having mended her glove, Minnie Marsh lays it in the drawer. She shuts the drawer with decision. I catch sight of her face in the glass. Lips are pursed. Chin held high. Next she laces her shoes. Then she touches her throat. What's your brooch? Mistletoe or merry-thought? And what is happening? Unless I'm much mistaken, the pulse's quickened, the moment's coming, the threads are racing, Niagara's ahead. Here's the crisis! Heaven be with you! Down she goes. Courage, courage! Face it, be it! For God's sake don't wait on the mat now! There's the door! I'm on your side. Speak! Confront her, confound her soul!

"Oh, I beg your pardon! Yes, this is Eastbourne. I'll reach it down for you. Let me try the handle." [But, Minnie, though we keep up pretences, I've read you rightI'm with you now].

"That's all your luggage?"

"Much obliged, I'm sure."

(But why do you look about you? Hilda won't come to the station, nor John; and Moggridge is driving at the far side of Eastbourne).

"I'll wait by my bag, ma'am, that's safest. He said he'd meet me....Oh, there he is! That's my son."

So they walked off together.

Well, but I'm confounded....Surely, Minnie, you know better! A strange young man....Stop! I'll tell himMinnie! Miss Marsh!I don't know though. There's something queer in her cloak as it blows. Oh, but it's untrue; it's indecent....Look how he bends as they reach the gateway. She finds her ticket. What's the joke? Off they go, down the road, side by side....Well, my world's done for! What do I stand on? What do I know? That's not Minnie. There never was Moggridge. Who am I? Life's bare as bone.

And yet the last look of themhe stepping from the kerb and she following him round the edge of the big building brims me with wonderfloods me anew. Mysterious figures! Mother and son. Who are you? Why do you walk down the street? Where to-night will you sleep, and then, to-morrow? Oh, how it whirls and surgesfloats me afresh! I start after them. People drive this way and that. The white light splutters and pours. Plate-glass windows. Carnations; chrysanthemums. Ivy in dark gardens. Milk carts at the door. Wherever I go, mysterious figures, I see you, turning the corner, mothers and sons; you, you, you. I hasten, I follow. This, I fancy, must be the sea. Grey is the landscape; dim as ashes; the water murmurs and moves. If I fall on my knees, if I go through the ritual, the ancient antics, it's you, unknown figures, you I adore; if I open my arms, it's you I embrace, you I draw to me adorable world!

# A Society

THIS IS HOW it all came about. Six or seven of us were sitting one day after tea. Some were gazing across the street into the windows of a milliner's shop where the light still shone brightly upon scarlet feathers and golden slippers. Others were idly occupied in building little towers of sugar upon the edge of the tea tray. After a time, so far as I can remember, we drew round the fire and began as usual to praise men—how strong, how noble, how brilliant, how courageous, how beautiful they were—how we envied those who by hook or by crook managed to get attached to one for life—when Poll, who had said nothing, burst into tears. Poll, I must tell you, has always been queer. For one thing her father was a strange man. He left her a fortune in his will, but on condition that she read all the books in the London Library. We comforted her as best we could; but we knew in our hearts how vain it was. For though we like her, Poll is no beauty; leaves her shoe laces untied; and must have been thinking, while we praised men, that not one of them would ever wish to marry her. At last she dried her tears. For some time we could make nothing of what she said. Strange enough it was in all conscience. She told us that, as we knew, she spent most of her time in the London Library, reading. She had begun, she said, with English literature on the top floor; and was steadily working her way down to the Times on the bottom. And now half, or perhaps only a quarter, way through a terrible thing had happened. She could read no more. Books were not what we thought them. "Books," she cried, rising to her feet and speaking with an intensity of desolation which I shall never forget, "are for the most part unutterably bad!"

Of course we cried out that Shakespeare wrote books, and Milton and Shelley.

"Oh, yes," she interrupted us. "You've been well taught, I can see. But you are not members of the London Library." Here her sobs broke forth anew. At length, recovering a little, she opened one of the pile of books which she always carried about with her"From a Window" or "In a Garden," or some such name as that it was called, and it was written by a man called Benton or Henson, or something of that kind. She read the first few pages. We listened in silence. "But that's not a book," someone said. So she chose another. This time it was a history, but I have forgotten the writer's name. Our trepidation increased as she went on. Not a word of it seemed to be true, and the style in which it was written was execrable.

"Poetry! Poetry!" we cried, impatiently. "Read us poetry!" I cannot describe the desolation which fell upon us as she opened a little volume and mouthed out the verbose, sentimental foolery which it contained.

"It must have been written by a woman," one of us urged. But no. She told us that it was written by a young man, one of the most famous poets of the day. I leave you to imagine what the shock of the discovery was. Though we all cried and begged her to read no more, she persisted and read us extracts from the Lives of the Lord Chancellors. When she had finished, Jane, the eldest and wisest of us, rose to her feet and said that she for one was not convinced.

"Why," she asked, "if men write such rubbish as this, should our mothers have wasted their youth in bringing them into the world?"

We were all silent; and, in the silence, poor Poll could be heard sobbing out, "Why, why did my father teach me to read?"

Clorinda was the first to come to her senses. "It's all our fault," she said. "Every one of us knows how to read. But no one, save Poll, has ever taken the trouble to do it. I, for one, have taken it for granted that it was a woman's duty to spend her youth in bearing children. I venerated my mother for bearing ten; still more my grandmother for bearing fifteen; it was, I confess, my own ambition to bear twenty. We have gone on all these ages supposing that men were equally industrious, and that their works were of equal merit. While we have borne the children, they, we supposed, have borne the books and the pictures. We have populated the world. They have civilized it. But now that we can read, what prevents us from judging the results? Before we bring another child into the world we must swear that we will find out what the world is like."

So we made ourselves into a society for asking questions. One of us was to visit a man-of-war; another was to hide herself in a scholar's study; another was to attend a meeting of business men; while all were to read books, look at pictures, go to concerts, keep our eyes open in the streets, and ask questions perpetually. We were very young. You can judge of our simplicity when I tell you that before parting that night we agreed that the objects of life were to produce good people and good books. Our questions were to be directed to finding out how far these objects were now attained by men. We vowed solemnly that we would not bear a single child until we were satisfied.

Off we went then, some to the British Museum; others to the King's Navy; some to Oxford; others to Cambridge; we visited the Royal Academy and the Tate; heard modern music in concert rooms, went to the Law courts, and saw new plays. No one dined out without asking her partner certain questions and carefully noting his replies. At intervals we met together and compared our observations. Oh, those were merry meetings! Never have I laughed so much as I did when Rose read her notes upon "Honour" and described how she had dressed herself as an thiopian Prince and gone abroad one of His Majesty's ships. Discovering the hoax, the Captain visited her (now disguised as a private gentleman) and demanded that honour should be satisfied. "But how?" she asked. "How?" he bellowed. "With the cane of course!" Seeing that he was beside himself with rage and expecting that her last moment had come, she bent over and received, to her amazement, six light taps upon the behind. "The honour of the British Navy is avenged!" he cried, and, raising herself, she saw him with the sweat pouring down his face holding out a trembling right hand. "Away!" she exclaimed, striking an attitude and imitating the ferocity of his own expression, "My hounour has still to be satisfied!" "Spoken like a gentleman!" he returned, and fell into profound thought. "If six strokes avenge the honour of the King's Navy, " he mused, "how many avenge the honour of a private gentleman?" He said he would prefer to lay the case before his brother officers. She replied haughtily that she could not wait. He praised her sensibility. "Let me see," he cried suddenly, "did your father keep a carriage?" "No," she said. "Or a riding horse?" "We had a donkey," she bethought her, "which drew the mowing machine." At this his face lighted. "My mother's name" she added. "For God's sake, man, don't mention your mother's name!" he shrieked, trembling like an aspen and flushing to the roots of his hair, and it was ten minutes at least before she could induce him to proceed. At length he decreed that if she gave him four strokes and a half in the small of the back at a spot indicated by himself (the half conceded, he said, in recognition of the fact that her great grandmother's uncle was killed at Trafalgar) it was his opinion that her honour would be as good as new. This was done; they retired to a restaurant; drank two bottles of wine for which he insisted upon paying; and parted with protestations of eternal friendship.

Then we had Fanny's account of her visit to the Law Courts. At her first visit she had come to the conclusion that the Judges were either made of wood or were impersonated by large animals resembling man who had been trained to move



A Haunted House and other writings

with extreme dignity, mumble and nod their heads. To test her theory she had liberated a handkerchief of bluebottles at the critical moment of a trial, but was unable to judge whether the creatures gave signs of humanity for the buzzing of the flies induced so sound a sleep that she only woke in time to see the prisoners led into the cells below. But from the evidence she brought we voted that it is unfair to suppose that the Judges are men.

Helen went to the Royal Academy, but when asked to deliver her report upon the pictures she began to recite from a pale blue volume, "O! for the touch of a vanished hand and the sound of a voice that is still. Home is the hunter, home from the hill. He gave his bridle reins a shake. Love is sweet, love is brief. Spring, the fair spring, is the year's pleasant King. O! to be in England now that April's there. Men must work and women must weep. The path of duty is the way to glory" We could listen to no more of this gibberish.

"We want no more poetry!" we cried.

"Daughters of England!" she began, but here we pulled her down, a vase of water getting spilt over her in the scuffle.

"Thank God!" she exclaimed, shaking herself like a dog. "Now I'll roll on the carpet and see if I can't brush off what remains of the Union Jack. Then perhaps" here she rolled energetically. Getting up she began to explain to us what modern pictures are like when Castalia stopped her.

"What is the average size of a picture?" she asked. "Perhaps two feet by two and a half," she said. Castalia made notes while Helen spoke, and when she had done, and we were trying not to meet each other's eyes, rose and said, "At your wish I spent last week at Oxbridge, disguised as a charwoman. I thus had access to the rooms of several Professors and will now attempt to give you some ideaonly," she broke off, "I can't think how to do it. It's all so queer. These Professors," she went on, "live in large houses built round grass plots each in a kind of cell by himself. Yet they have every convenience and comfort. You have only to press a button or light a little lamp. Their papers are beautifully filed. Books abound. There are no children or animals, save half a dozen stray cats and one aged bullfincha cock. I remember," she broke off, "an Aunt of mine who lived at Dulwich and keep cactuses. You reached the conservatory through the double drawing-room, and there, on the hot pipes, were dozens of them, ugly, squat, bristly little plants each in a separate pot. Once in a hundred years the Aloe flowered, so my Aunt said. But she died before that happened" We told her to keep to the point. "Well," she resumed, "when Professor Hobkin was out, I examined his life work, an edition of Sappho. It's a queer looking book, six or seven inches thick, not all by Sappho. Oh, no. Most of it is a defence of Sappho's chastity, which some German had denied, and I can assure you the passion with which these two gentlemen argued, the learning they displayed, the prodigious ingenuity with which they disputed the use of some implement which looked to me for all the world like a hairpin astounded me; especially when the door opened and Professor Hobkin himself appeared. A very nice, mild, old gentleman, but what could he know about chastity?" We misunderstood her.

"No, no," she protested, "he's the soul of honour I'm surenot that he resembles Rose's sea captain in the least. I was thinking rather of my aunt's cactuses. What could they know about chastity?"

Again we told her not to wander from the point,did the Oxbridge professors help to produce good people and good books?the objects of life.

"There!" she exclaimed. "It never struck me to ask. It never occurred to me that they could possibly produce anything."

"I believe," said Sue, "that you made some mistake.

Probably Professor Hobkin was a gyncologist. A scholar is overflowing with humour and inventionperhaps addicted to wine, but what of that?a delightful companion, generous, subtle, imaginativeas stands to reason. For he spends his life in company with the finest human beings that have ever existed.”

“Hum,” said Castalia. “Perhaps I’d better go back and try again.”

Some three months later it happened that I was sitting alone when Castalia entered. I don’t know what it was in the look of her that so moved me; but I could not restrain myself, and, dashing across the room, I clasped her in my arms. Not only was she very beautiful; she seemed also in the highest spirits. “How happy you look!” I exclaimed, as she sat down.

“I’ve been at Oxbridge,” she said.

“Asking questions?”

“Answering them,” she replied.

“You have not broken our vow?” I said anxiously, noticing something about her figure.

“Oh, the vow,” she said casually. “I’m going to have a baby, if that’s what you mean. You can’t imagine,” she burst out, “how exciting, how beautiful, how satisfying”

“What is?” I asked.

“Totoanswer questions,” she replied in some confusion. Whereupon she told me the whole of her story. But in the middle of an account which interested and excited me more than anything I had ever heard, she gave the strangest cry, half whoop, half holloa

“Chastity! Chastity! Where’s my chastity!” she cried. “Help Ho! The scent bottle!”

There was nothing in the room but a cruet contained mustard, which I was about to administer when she recovered her composure.

"You should have thought of that three months ago," I said severely.

"True," she replied. "There's not much good in thinking of it now. It was unfortunate, by the way, that my mother had me called Castalia."

"Oh, Castalia, your mother" I was beginning when she reached for the mustard pot.

"No, no, no," she said, shaking her head. "If you'd been a chaste woman yourself you would have screamed at the sight of meinstead of which you rushed across the room and took me in your arms. No, Cassandra. We are neither of us chaste." So we went on talking.

Meanwhile the room was filling up, for it was the day appointed to discuss the results of our observations. Everyone, I thought, felt as I did about Castalia. They kissed her and said how glad they were to see her again. At length, when we were all assembled, Jane rose and said that it was time to begin. She began by saying that we had now asked questions for over five years, and that though the results were bound to be inconclusivehere Castalia nudged me and whispered that she was not so sure about that. Then she got up, and interrupting Jane in the middle of a sentence, said:

"Before you say any more, I want to knowam I to stay in the room? Because," she added, "I have to confess that I am an impure woman."

Everyone looked at her in astonishment.

"You are going to have a baby?" asked Jane.

She nodded her head.

It was extraordinary to see the different expressions on their faces. A sort of hum went through the room in which I could catch the words "impure," and "baby," "Castalia," and so on. Jane, who was herself considerably moved, put it to us:

"Shall she go? Is she impure?"

Such a roar filled the room as might have been heard in the street outside.

"No! No! No! Let her stay! Impure? Fiddlesticks!" Yet I fancied that some of the youngest, girls of nineteen or twenty, held back as if overcome with shyness. Then we all came about her and began asking questions, and at last I saw one of the youngest, who had kept in the background, approach shyly and say to her:

"What is chastity then? I mean is it good, or is it bad, or is it nothing at all?" She replied so low that I could not catch what she said.

"You know I was shocked," said another, "for at least ten minutes."

"In my opinion," said Poll, who was growing crusty from always reading in the London Library, "chastity is nothing but ignorancea most discreditable state of mind. We should admit only the unchaste to our society. I vote that Castalia shall be our President."

This was violently disputed.

"It is as unfair to brand women with chastity as with unchastity," said Poll. "Some of us haven't the opportunity either. Moreover, I don't believe Cassy herself maintains that she acted as she did from a pure love of knowledge."

"He is only twenty-one and divinely beautiful," said Cassy, with a ravishing gesture.

"I move," said Helen, "that no one be allowed to talk of chastity or unchastity save those who are in love."

"Oh, bother," said Judith, who had been enquiring into

scientific matters, "I'm not in love and I'm longing to explain my measures for dispensing with prostitutes and fertilizing virgins by Act of Parliament."

She went on to tell us of an invention of hers to be erected at Tube stations and other public resorts, which, upon payment of a small fee, would safeguard the nation's health, accommodate its sons, and relieve its daughters. Then she had contrived a method of preserving in sealed tubes the germs of future Lord Chancellors "or poets or painters or musicians," she went on, "supposing, that is to say, that these breeds are not extinct, and that women still wish to bear children"

"Of course we wish to bear children!" cried Castalia, impatiently. Jane rapped the table.

"That is the very point we are met to consider," she said. "For five years we have been trying to find out whether we are justified in continuing the human race. Castalia has anticipated our decision. But it remains for the rest of us to make up our minds."

Here one after another of our messengers rose and delivered their reports. The marvels of civilisation far exceeded our expectations, and, as we learnt for the first time how man flies in the air, talks across space, penetrates to the heart of an atom, and embraces the universe in his speculations, a murmur of admiration burst from our lips.

"We are proud," we cried, "that our mothers sacrificed their youth in such a cause as this!" Castalia, who had been listening intently, looked prouder than all the rest. Then Jane reminded us that we had still much to learn, and Castalia begged us to make haste. On we went through a vast tangle of statistics. We learnt that England has a population of so many millions, and that such and such a proportion of them is constantly hungry and in prison; that the average size of a working man's family is such, and that so great a percentage of women die from maladies incident to childbirth. Reports were read of visits to factories, shops, slums, and dockyards. Descriptions were given of the Stock Exchange, of a gigantic house of business in the City, and of a Government Office. The British Colonies were now discussed, and some account was given to our rule in India, Africa and Ireland. I was sitting by Castalia and I noticed her uneasiness.

"We shall never come by any conclusion at all at this rate," she said. "As it appears that civilisation is so much more complex than we had any notion, would it not be better to confine ourselves to our original enquiry? We agreed that it was the object of life to produce good people and good books. All this time we have been talking of aeroplanes, factories, and money. Let us talk about men themselves and their arts, for that is the heart of the matter."

So the diners out stepped forward with long slips of paper containing answers to their questions. These had been framed after much consideration. A good man, we had agreed, must at any rate be honest, passionate, and unworldly. But whether or not a particular man possessed those qualities could only be discovered by asking questions, often beginning at a remote distance from the centre. Is Kensington a nice place to live in? Where is your son being educatedand your daughter? Now please tell me, what do you pay for your cigars? By the way, is Sir Joseph a baronet or only a knight? Often it seemed that we learnt more from trivial questions of this kind than from more direct ones. "I accepted my peerage," said Lord Bunkum, "because my wife wished it." I forget how many titles were accepted for the same reason. "Working fifteen hours out of the twenty-four, as I do" ten thousand professional men began.

"No, no, of course you can neither read nor write. But why do you work so hard?" "My dear lady, with a growing family" "But why does your family grow?" Their wives wished that too, or perhaps it was the British Empire. But more significant than the answers were the refusals to answer. Very few would reply at all to questions about morality and religion, and such answers as were given were not serious. Questions as to the value of money and power were almost invariably brushed aside, or pressed at extreme risk to the asker. "I'm sure," said Jill, "that if Sir Harley Tightboots hadn't been carving the mutton when I asked him about the capitalist system he would have cut my throat. The only reason why we escaped with our lives over and over again is that men are at once so hungry and so chivalrous. They despise us too much to mind what we say."

"Of course they despise us," said Eleanor. "As the same time how do you account for thisI made enquiries among the artists. Now, no woman has ever been an artist, has she, Poll?"

"Jane-Austen-Charlotte-Bront-George-Eliot," cried Poll, like a man crying muffins in a back street.

"Damn the woman!" someone exclaimed. "What a bore she is!"

"Since Sappho there has been no female of first rate" Eleanor began, quoting from a weekly newspaper.

"It's now well known that Sappho was the somewhat lewd invention of Professor Hobkin," Ruth interrupted.

"Anyhow, there is no reason to suppose that any woman ever has been able to write or ever will be able to write," Eleanor continued. "And yet, whenever I go among authors they never cease to talk to me about their books. Masterly! I say, or Shakespeare himself! (for one must say something) and I assure you, they believe me."

"That proves nothing," said Jane. "They all do it. Only," she signed, "it doesn't seem to help us much. Perhaps we had better examine modern literature next. Liz, it's your turn."

Elizabeth rose and said that in order to prosecute her enquiry she had dressed as a man and been taken for a reviewer.

                    A Haunted House and other writings

"I have read new books pretty steadily for the past five years," said she. "Mr. Wells is the most popular living writer; then comes Mr. Arnold Bennett; then Mr. Compton Mackenzie; Mr. McKenna and Mr. Walpole may be bracketed together." She sat down.

"But you've told us nothing!" we expostulated. "Or do you mean that these gentlemen have greatly surpassed Jane-Eliot and that English fiction iswhere's that review of yours? Oh, yes, 'safe in their hands.'"

"Safe, quite safe," she said, shifting uneasily from foot to foot. "And I'm sure that they give away even more than they receive."

We were all sure of that. "But," we pressed her, "do they write good books?"

"Good books?" she said, looking at the ceiling. "You must remember," she began, speaking with extreme rapidity, "that fiction is the mirror of life. And you can't deny that education is of the highest importance, and that it would be extremely annoying, if you found yourself alone at Brighton late at night, not to know which was the best boarding house to stay at, and suppose it was a dripping Sunday eveningwouldn't it be nice to go to the Movies?"

"But what has that got to do with it?" we asked.

"Nothingnothingnothing whatever," she replied.

"Well, tell us the truth," we bade her.

"The truth? But isn't it wonderful," she broke off"Mr. Chitter has written a weekly article for the past thirty years upon love or hot buttered toast and has sent all his sons to Eton"

"The truth!" we demanded.

"Oh, the truth," she stammered, "the truth has nothing to

do with literature," and sitting down she refused to say another word.

It all seemed to us very inconclusive.

"Ladies, we must try to sum up the results," Jane was beginning, when a hum, which had been heard for some time through the open window, drowned her voice.

"War! War! War! Declaration of War!" men were shouting in the street below.

We looked at each other in horror.

"What war?" we cried. "What war?" We remembered, too late, that we had never thought of sending anyone to the House of Commons. We had forgotten all about it. We turned to Poll, who had reached the history shelves in the London Library, and asked her to enlighten us.

"Why," we cried, "do men go to war?"

"Sometimes for one reason, sometimes for another," she replied calmly. "In 1760, for example" The shouts outside drowned her words. "Again in 1797in 1804It was the Austrians in 18661870 was the Franco-PrussianIn 1900 on the other hand"

"But it's now 1914!" we cut her short.

"Ah, I don't know what they're going to war for now," she admitted.

* * * * *

The war was over and peace was in process of being signed, when I once more found myself with Castalia in the room where our meetings used to be held. We began idly turning over the pages of our old minute books. "Queer," I mused, "to see what we were thinking five years ago." "We are agreed," Castalia quoted, reading over my shoulder, "that it is the object of life to produce good people and good books." We made

     A Haunted House and other writings

no comment upon that. "A good man is at any rate honest, passionate and unworldly." "What a woman's language!" I observed. "Oh, dear," cried Castalia, pushing the book away from her, "what fools we were! It was all Poll's father's fault," she went on. "I believe he did it on purposethat ridiculous will, I mean, forcing Poll to read all the books in the London Library. If we hadn't learnt to read," she said bitterly, "we might still have been bearing children in ignorance and that I believe was the happiest life after all. I know what you're going to say about war," she checked me, "and the horror of bearing children to see them killed, but our mothers did it, and their mothers, and their mothers before them. And they didn't complain. They couldn't read. I've done my best," she sighed, "to prevent my little girl from learning to read, but what's the use? I caught Ann only yesterday with a newspaper in her hand and she was beginning to ask me if it was 'true.' Next she'll ask me whether Mr. Lloyd George is a good man, then whether Mr. Arnold Bennett is a good novelist, and finally whether I believe in God. How can I bring my daughter up to believe in nothing?" she demanded.

"Surely you could teach her to believe that a man's intellect is, and always will be, fundamentally superior to a woman's?" I suggested. She brightened at this and began to turn over our old minutes again. "Yes," she said, "think of their discoveries, their mathematics, their science, their philosophy, their scholarship" and then she began to laugh, "I shall never forget old Hobkin and the hairpin," she said, and went on reading and laughing and I thought she was quite happy, when suddenly she drew the book from her and burst out, "Oh, Cassandra, why do you torment me? Don't you know that our belief in man's intellect is the greatest fallacy of them all?" "What?" I exclaimed. "Ask any journalist, schoolmaster, politician or public house keeper in the land and they will all tell you that men are much cleverer than women." "As if I doubted it," she said scornfully. "How could they help it? Haven't we bred them and fed and kept them in comfort since the beginning of time so that they may be clever even if they're nothing else? It's all our doing!" she cried. "We insisted upon having intellect and now we've got it. And it's intellect," she continued, "that's at the bottom of it. What could be more charming than a boy before he has begun to cultivate his intellect? He is beautiful to look at; he gives himself no airs; he understand the meaning of art and literature instinctively; he goes about enjoying his life and making other people enjoy theirs. Then they teach him to cultivate his intellect. He becomes a barrister, a civil servant, a general, an author, a professor. Every day he goes to an office. Every year he produces a book. He maintains a whole family by the products of his brainpoor devil! Soon he cannot come into a room without making us all feel uncomfortable; he condescends to every woman he meets, and dares not tell the truth even to his own wife; instead of rejoicing our eyes we have to shut them if we are to take him in our arms. True, they console themselves with stars of all shapes, ribbons of all shades, and incomes of all sizesbut what is to console us? That we shall be able in ten years' time to spend a week-end at Lahore? Or that the least insect in Japan has a name twice the length of its body? Oh, Cassandra, for Heaven's sake let us devise a method by which men may bear children! It is our only chance. For unless we provide them with some innocent occupation we shall get neither good people nor good books; we shall perish beneath the fruits of their unbridled activity; and not a human being will survive to know that there once was Shakespeare!"

"It is too late," I replied. "We cannot provide even for the children that we have."

"And then you ask me to believe in intellect," she said.

While we spoke, men were crying hoarsely and wearily in the street, and, listening, we heard that the Treaty of Peace had just been signed. The voices died away. The rain was falling and

                    A Haunted House and other writings

interfered no doubt with the proper explosion of the fireworks.

"My cook will have bought the Evening News," said Castalia, "and Ann will be spelling it out over her tea. I must go home."

"It's no good—not a bit of good," I said. "Once she knows how to read there's only one thing you can teach her to believe in—and that is herself."

"Well, that would be a change," sighed Castalia.

So we swept up the papers of our Society, and, though Ann was playing with her doll very happily, we solemnly made her a present of the lot and told her we had chosen her to be President of the Society of the future—upon which she burst into tears, poor little girl.

# Blue & Green

GREEN THE POINTED FINGERS of glass hang downwards. The light slides down the glass, and drops a pool of green. All day long the ten fingers of the lustre drop green upon the marble. The feathers of parakeetstheir harsh criessharp blades of palm treesgreen, too; green needles glittering in the sun. But the hard glass drips on to the marble; the pools hover above the desert sand; the camels lurch through them; the pools settle on the marble; rushes edge them; weeds clog them; here and there a white blossom; the frog flops over; at night the stars are set there unbroken. Evening comes, and the shadow sweeps the green over the mantlepiece; the ruffled surface of ocean. No ships come; the aimless waves sway beneath the empty sky. It's night; the needles drip blots of blue. The green's out.

BLUE The snub-nosed monster rises to the surface and spouts through his blunt nostrils two columns of water, which, fiery-white in the centre, spray off into a fringe of blue beads. Strokes of blue line the black tarpaulin of his hide. Slushing the water through mouth and nostrils he sings, heavy with water, and the blue closes over him dowsing the polished pebbles of his eyes. Thrown upon the beach he lies, blunt, obtuse, shedding dry blue scales. Their metallic blue stains the rusty iron on the beach. Blue are the ribs of the wrecked rowing boat. A wave rolls beneath the blue bells. But the cathedral's different, cold, incense laden, faint blue with the veils of madonnas.

                              A Haunted House and other writings

# In the Orchard

Miranda slept in the orchard, lying in a long chair beneath the apple tree. Her book had fallen into the grass, and her finger still seemed to point at the sentence: 'Ce pays est vraiment un des coins du monde oui le rire des filles elate le mieux . . .'* as if she had fallen asleep just there. The opals on her finger flushed green, flushed rosy, and again flushed orange as the sun, oozing through the apple-trees, filled them. Then, when the breeze blew, her purple dress rippled like a flower attached to a stalk; the grasses nodded; and the white butterfly came blowing this way and that just above her face.

Four feet in the air over her head the apples hung. Suddenly there was a shrill clamour as if they were gongs of cracked brass beaten violently, irregularly, and brutally. It was only the school-children saying the multiplication table in unison, stopped by the teacher, scolded, and beginning to say the multiplication table over again. But this clamour passed four feet above Miranda's head, went through the apple boughs, and, striking against the cowman's little boy who was picking blackberries in the hedge when he should have been at school, made him tear his thumb on the thorns.

Next there was a solitary cry--sad, human, brutal. Old Parsley was, indeed, blind drunk.

Then the very topmost leaves of the apple-tree, flat like little fish against the blue, thirty feet above the earth, chimed with a pensive and lugubrious note. It was the organ in the church playing one of Hymns Ancient and Modern. The sound floated out and was cut into atoms by a flock of field-fares flying at an enormous speed--somewhere or other. Miranda lay asleep thirty feet beneath.

Then above the apple-tree and the pear-tree two hundred feet above Miranda lying asleep in the orchard bells thudded, intermittent, sullen, didactic, for six poor women of the parish were being churched and the Rector was returning thanks to heaven.

And above that with a sharp squeak the golden feather of the church tower turned from south to east. The wind changed. Above everything else it droned, above the woods, the meadows, the hills, miles above Miranda lying in the orchard asleep. It swept on, eyeless, brainless, meeting nothing that could stand against it, until, wheeling the other way, it turned south again. Miles below, in a space as big as the eye of a needle, Miranda stood upright and cried aloud: 'Oh, I shall be late for tea!'

Miranda slept in the orchard--or perhaps she was not asleep, for her lips moved very slightly as if they were saying: 'Ce pays est vraiment un des coins du monde . . . oui le rire des filles . . . eclate . . . eclate . . . eclate.'** and then she smiled and let her body sink all its weight on to the enormous earth which rises, she thought, to carry me on its back as if I were a leaf, or a queen (here the children said the multiplication table), or, Miranda went on, I might be lying on the top of a cliff with the gulls screaming above me. The higher they fly, she continued, as the teacher scolded the children and rapped Jimmy over the knuckles till they bled, the deeper they look into the sea-- into the sea, she repeated, and her fingers relaxed and her lips closed gently as if she were floating on the sea, and then, when the shout of the drunken man sounded overhead, she drew breath with an extraordinary ecstasy, for she thought that she heard life itself crying out from a rough tongue in a scarlet mouth, from the wind, from the bells, from the curved green leaves of the cabbages.

Naturally she was being married when the organ played the tune from Hymns Ancient and Modern, and, when the bells rang after the six poor women had been churched, the sullen intermittent thud made her think that the very earth shook with the hoofs of the horse that was galloping towards her ('Ah, I have only to wait!' she sighed), and it seemed to her that everything had already begun moving, crying, riding, flying round her, across her, towards her in a pattern.

Mary is chopping the wood, she thought; Pearman is herding the cows; the carts are coming up from the meadows; the rider--and she traced out the lines that the men, the carts, the birds, and the rider made over the countryside until they all seemed driven out, round, and across by the beat of her own heart.

Miles up in the air the wind changed; the golden feather of the church tower squeaked; and Miranda jumped up and cried: 'Oh, I shall be late for tea!'

Miranda slept in the orchard, or was she asleep or was she not asleep? Her purple dress stretched between the two apple-trees. There were twenty-four apple-trees in the orchard, some slanting slightly, others growing straight with a rush up the trunk which spread wide into branches and formed into round red or yellow drops. Each apple-tree had sufficient space. The sky exactly fitted the leaves. When the breeze blew, the line of the boughs against the wall slanted slightly and then returned. A wagtail flew diagonally from one corner to another. Cautiously hopping, a thrush advanced towards a fallen apple; from the other wall a sparrow fluttered just above the grass. The uprush of the trees was tied down by these movements; the whole was compacted by the orchard walls. For miles beneath the earth was clamped together; rippled on the surface with wavering air; and across the corner of the orchard the blue-green was slit by a purple streak. The wind changing, one bunch of apples was tossed so high that it blotted out two cows in the meadow ('Oh, I shall be late for tea!' cried Miranda), and the apples hung straight across the wall again.

# Kew Gardens

FROM THE OVAL-SHAPED flower-bed there rose perhaps a hundred stalks spreading into heart-shaped or tongue-shaped leaves half way up and unfurling at the tip red or blue or yellow petals marked with spots of colour raised upon the surface; and from the red, blue or yellow gloom of the throat emerged a straight bar, rough with gold dust and slightly clubbed at the end. The petals were voluminous enough to be stirred by the summer breeze, and when they moved, the red, blue and yellow lights passed one over the other, staining an inch of the brown earth beneath with a spot of the most intricate colour. The light fell either upon the smooth, grey back of a pebble, or, the shell of a snail with its brown, circular veins, or falling into a raindrop, it expanded with such intensity of red, blue and yellow the thin walls of water that one expected them to burst and disappear. Instead, the drop was left in a second silver grey once more, and the light now settled upon the flesh of a leaf, revealing the branching thread of fibre beneath the surface, and again it moved on and spread its illumination in the vast green spaces beneath the dome of the heart-shaped and tongue-shaped leaves. Then the breeze stirred rather more briskly overhead and the colour was flashed into the air above, into the eyes of the men and women who walk in Kew Gardens in July.

The figures of these men and women straggled past the flower-bed with a curiously irregular movement not unlike that of the white and blue butterflies who crossed the turf in zig-zag flights from bed to bed. The man was about six inches in front of the woman, strolling carelessly, while she bore on with greater purpose, only turning her head now and then to see that the children were not too far behind. The man kept this distance in front of the woman purposely, though perhaps unconsciously, for he wished to go on with his thoughts.

"Fifteen years ago I came here with Lily," he thought. "We sat somewhere over there by a lake and I begged her to marry me all through the hot afternoon. How the dragonfly kept circling round us: how clearly I see the dragonfly and her shoe with the square silver buckle at the toe. All the time I spoke I saw her shoe and when it moved impatiently I knew without looking up what she was going to say: the whole of her seemed to be in her shoe. And my love, my desire, were in the dragonfly; for some reason I thought that if it settled there, on that leaf, the broad one with the red flower in the middle of it, if the dragonfly settled on the leaf she would say 'Yes' at once. But the dragonfly went round and round: it never settled anywhereof course not, happily not, or I shouldn't be walking here with Eleanor and the children. "Tell me, Eleanor. D'you ever think of the past?"

"Why do you ask, Simon?"

"Because I've been thinking of the past. I've been thinking of Lily, the woman I might have married.... Well, why are you silent? Do you mind my thinking of the past?"

"Why should I mind, Simon? Doesn't one always think of the past, in a garden with men and women lying under the trees? Aren't they one's past, all that remains of it, those men and women, those ghosts lying under the trees,... one's happiness, one's reality?"

"For me, a square silver shoe buckle and a dragonfly"

"For me, a kiss. Imagine six little girls sitting before their easels twenty years ago, down by the side of a lake, painting the water-lilies, the first red water-lilies I'd ever seen. And suddenly a kiss, there on the back of my neck. And my hand shook all the afternoon so that I couldn't paint. I took out my watch and marked the hour when I would allow myself to think of the kiss for five minutes onlyit was so preciousthe kiss of an old grey-haired woman with a wart on her nose, the mother of all my kisses all my life. Come, Caroline, come, Hubert."

They walked on the past the flower-bed, now walking four abreast, and soon diminished in size among the trees and looked half transparent as the sunlight and shade swam over their backs in large trembling irregular patches.

In the oval flower bed the snail, whose shell had been stained red, blue, and yellow for the space of two minutes or so, now appeared to be moving very slightly in its shell, and next began to labour over the crumbs of loose earth which broke away and rolled down as it passed over them. It appeared to have a definite goal in front of it, differing in this respect from the singular high stepping angular green insect who attempted to cross in front of it, and waited for a second with its antenn trembling as if in deliberation, and then stepped off as rapidly and strangely in the opposite direction. Brown cliffs with deep green lakes in the hollows, flat, blade-like trees that waved from root to tip, round boulders of grey stone, vast crumpled surfaces of a thin crackling textureall these objects lay across the snail's progress between one stalk and another to his goal. Before he had decided whether to circumvent the arched tent of a dead leaf or to breast it there came past the bed the feet of other human beings.

This time they were both men. The younger of the two wore an expression of perhaps unnatural calm; he raised his eyes and fixed them very steadily in front of him while his companion spoke, and directly his companion had done speaking he looked on the ground again and sometimes opened his lips only after a long pause and sometimes did not open them at all. The elder man had a curiously uneven and shaky method of walking, jerking his hand forward and throwing up his head abruptly, rather in the manner of an impatient carriage horse tired of waiting outside a house; but in the man these gestures


A Haunted House and other writings

were irresolute and pointless. He talked almost incessantly; he smiled to himself and again began to talk, as if the smile had been an answer. He was talking about spiritsthe spirits of the dead, who, according to him, were even now telling him all sorts of odd things about their experiences in Heaven.

"Heaven was known to the ancients as Thessaly, William, and now, with this war, the spirit matter is rolling between the hills like thunder." He paused, seemed to listen, smiled, jerked his head and continued:

"You have a small electric battery and a piece of rubber to insulate the wireisolate?insulate?well, we'll skip the details, no good going into details that wouldn't be understoodand in short the little machine stands in any convenient position by the head of the bed, we will say, on a neat mahogany stand. All arrangements being properly fixed by workmen under my direction, the widow applies her ear and summons the spirit by sign as agreed. Women! Widows! Women in black"

Here he seemed to have caught sight of a woman's dress in the distance, which in the shade looked a purple black. He took off his hat, placed his hand upon his heart, and hurried towards her muttering and gesticulating feverishly. But William caught him by the sleeve and touched a flower with the tip of his walking-stick in order to divert the old man's attention. After looking at it for a moment in some confusion the old man bent his ear to it and seemed to answer a voice speaking from it, for he began talking about the forests of Uruguay which he had visited hundreds of years ago in company with the most beautiful young woman in Europe. He could be heard murmuring about forests of Uruguay blanketed with the wax petals of tropical roses, nightingales, sea beaches, mermaids, and women drowned at sea, as he suffered himself to be moved on by William, upon whose face the look of stoical patience grew slowly deeper and deeper.

Following his steps so closely as to be slightly puzzled

by his gestures came two elderly women of the lower middle class, one stout and ponderous, the other rosy cheeked and nimble. Like most people of their station they were frankly fascinated by any signs of eccentricity betokening a disordered brain, especially in the well-to-do; but they were too far off to be certain whether the gestures were merely eccentric or genuinely mad. After they had scrutinised the old man's back in silence for a moment and given each other a queer, sly look, they went on energetically piecing together their very complicated dialogue:

"Nell, Bert, Lot, Cess, Phil, Pa, he says, I says, she says, I says, I says, I says"

"My Bert, Sis, Bill, Grandad, the old man, sugar,

Sugar, flour, kippers, greens, Sugar, sugar, sugar." The ponderous woman looked through the pattern of falling words at the flowers standing cool, firm, and upright in the earth, with a curious expression. She saw them as a sleeper waking from a heavy sleep sees a brass candlestick reflecting the light in an unfamiliar way, and closes his eyes and opens them, and seeing the brass candlestick again, finally starts broad awake and stares at the candlestick with all his powers. So the heavy woman came to a standstill opposite the oval-shaped flower bed, and ceased even to pretend to listen to what the other woman was saying. She stood there letting the words fall over her, swaying the top part of her body slowly backwards and forwards, looking at the flowers. Then she suggested that they should find a seat and have their tea. The snail had now considered every possible method of reaching his goal without going round the dead leaf or climbing over it. Let alone the effort needed for climbing a leaf, he was doubtful whether the thin texture which vibrated with such an alarming crackle when touched even by the tip of his horns would bear his weight; and this determined him finally to creep beneath it, for there was a point where the leaf curved high enough from the ground to admit him. He had just inserted his head in the opening and was taking stock of the high brown roof and was getting used to the cool brown light when two other people came past outside on the turf. This time they were both young, a young man and a young woman. They were both in the prime of youth, or even in that season which precedes the prime of youth, the season before the smooth pink folds of the flower have burst their gummy case, when the wings of the butterfly, though fully grown, are motionless in the sun.

"Lucky it isn't Friday," he observed.

"Why? D'you believe in luck?"

"They make you pay sixpence on Friday."

"What's sixpence anyway? Isn't it worth sixpence?"

"What's 'it'what do you mean by 'it'?"

"O, anythingI meanyou know what I mean."

Long pauses came between each of these remarks; they were uttered in toneless and monotonous voices. The couple stood still on the edge of the flower bed, and together pressed the end of her parasol deep down into the soft earth. The action and the fact that his hand rested on the top of hers expressed their feelings in a strange way, as these short insignificant words also expressed something, words with short wings for their heavy body of meaning, inadequate to carry them far and thus alighting awkwardly upon the very common objects that surrounded them, and were to their inexperienced touch so massive; but who knows (so they thought as they pressed the parasol into the earth) what precipices aren't concealed in them, or what slopes of ice don't shine in the sun on the other side? Who knows? Who has ever seen this before? Even when she wondered what sort of tea they gave you at Kew, he felt that something loomed up behind her words, and stood vast and solid behind them; and the mist very slowly rose and uncovered. O, Heavens, what were those shapes? Little white tables, and waitresses who looked first at her and then at him; and there was a bill that he would pay with a real two shilling piece, and it was real, all real, he assured himself, fingering the coin in his pocket, real to everyone except to him and to her; even to him it began to seem real; and then but it was too exciting to stand and think any longer, and he pulled the parasol out of the earth with a jerk and was impatient to find the place where one had tea with other people, like other people.

"Come along, Trissie; it's time we had our tea."

"Wherever does one have one's tea?" she asked with the oddest thrill of excitement in her voice, looking vaguely round and letting herself be drawn on down the grass path, trailing her parasol, turning her head this way and that way, forgetting her tea, wishing to go down there and then down there, remembering orchids and cranes among wild flowers, a Chinese pagoda and a crimson crested bird; but he bore her on.

Thus one couple after another with much the same irregular and aimless movement passed the flower-bed and were enveloped in layer after layer of green blue vapour, in which at first their bodies had substance and a dash of colour, but later both substance and colour dissolved in the green-blue atmosphere. How hot it was! So hot that even the thrush chose to hop, like a mechanical bird, in the shadow of the flowers, with long pauses between one movement and the next; instead of rambling vaguely the white butterflies danced one above another, making with their white shifting flakes the outline of a shattered marble column above the tallest flowers; the glass roofs of the palm house shone as if a whole market full of shiny green umbrellas had opened in the sun; and in the drone of the aeroplane the voice of the summer sky murmured its fierce soul. Yellow and black, pink and snow white, shapes of all these colours, men, women, and children were spotted for a second upon the horizon, and then, seeing the breadth of yellow that lay upon the grass, they wavered and sought shade beneath the trees, dissolving like drops of water in the yellow and green atmosphere, staining it faintly with red and blue. It seemed as if all gross and heavy bodies had sunk down in the heat motionless and lay huddled upon the ground, but their voices went wavering from them as if they were flames lolling from the thick waxen bodies of candles. Voices. Yes, voices. Wordless voices, breaking the silence suddenly with such depth of contentment, such passion of desire, or, in the voices of children, such freshness of surprise; breaking the silence? But there was no silence; all the time the motor omnibuses were turning their wheels and changing their gear; like a vast nest of Chinese boxes all of wrought steel turning ceaselessly one within another the city murmured; on the top of which the voices cried aloud and the petals of myriads of flowers flashed their colours into the air.

# Monday Or Tuesday

LAZY AND INDIFFERENT, shaking space easily from his wings, knowing his way, the heron passes over the church beneath the sky. White and distant, absorbed in itself, endlessly the sky covers and uncovers, moves and remains. A lake? Blot the shores of it out! A mountain? Oh, perfect the sun gold on its slopes. Down that falls. Ferns then, or white feathers, for ever and ever--

Desiring truth, awaiting it, laboriously distilling a few words, for ever desiring—(a cry starts to the left, another to the right. Wheels strike divergently. Omnibuses conglomerate in conflict)—for ever desiring—(the clock asseverates with twelve distinct strokes that it is midday; light sheds gold scales; children swarm)—for ever desiring truth. Red is the dome; coins hang on the trees; smoke trails from the chimneys; bark, shout, cry "Iron for sale"—and truth?

Radiating to a point men's feet and women's feet, black or gold-encrusted—(This foggy weather—Sugar? No, thank you—The commonwealth of the future)—the firelight darting and making the room red, save for the black figures and their bright eyes, while outside a van discharges, Miss Thingummy drinks tea at her desk, and plate-glass preserves fur coats———

Flaunted, leaf-light, drifting at corners, blown across the wheels, silver-splashed, home or not home, gathered, scattered, squandered in separate scales, swept up, down, torn, sunk, assembled-- and truth?

Now to recollect by the fireside on the white square of marble. From ivory depths words rising shed their blackness, blossom and penetrate. Fallen the book; in the flame, in the smoke, in the momentary sparks-- or now voyaging, the marble square pendant, minarets beneath and the Indian seas, while space rushes blue and stars glint truth? Or now, content with closeness?

Lazy and indifferent the heron returns; the sky veils her stars; then bares them.

# Mr. Bennett and Mrs. Brown

It seems to me possible, perhaps desirable, that I may be the only person in this room who has committed the folly of writing, trying to write, or failing to write, a novel. And when I asked myself, as your invitation to speak to you about modern fiction made me ask myself, what demon whispered in my ear and urged me to my doom, a little figure rose before me— the figure of a man, or of a woman, who said, "My name is Brown. Catch me if you can."

Most novelists have the same experience. Some Brown, Smith, or Jones comes before them and says in the most seductive and charming way in the world, "Come and catch me if you can." And so, led on by this will-o'-the-wisp, they flounder through volume after volume, spending the best years of their lives in the pursuit, and receiving for the most part very little cash in exchange. Few catch the phantom; most have to be content with a scrap of her dress or a wisp of her hair.

My belief that men and women write novels because they are lured on to create some character which has thus imposed itself upon them has the sanction of Mr. Arnold Bennett. In an article from which I will quote he says: "The foundation of good fiction is character-creating and nothing else. . . . Style counts; plot counts; originality of outlook counts. But none of these counts anything like so much as the convincingness of the characters. If the characters are real the novel will have a chance; if they are not, oblivion will be its portion. . . ." And he goes on to draw the conclusion that we have no young novelists of first-rate importance at the present moment, because they are unable to create characters that are real, true, and convincing.

These are the questions that I want with greater boldness

   

than discretion to discuss to-night. I want to make out what we mean when we talk about "character" in fiction; to say something about the question of reality which Mr. Bennett raises; and to suggest some reasons why the younger novelists fail to create characters, if, as Mr. Bennett asserts, it is true that fail they do. This will lead me, I am well aware, to make some very sweeping and some very vague assertions. For the question is an extremely difficult one. Think how little we know about character—think how little we know about art. But, to make a clearance before I begin, I will suggest that we range Edwardians and Georgians into two camps; Mr. Wells, Mr. Bennett, and Mr. Galsworthy I will call the Edwardians; Mr. Forster, Mr. Lawrence, Mr. Strachey, Mr. Joyce, and Mr. Eliot I will call the Georgians. And if I speak in the first person, with intolerable egotism, I will ask you to excuse me. I do not want to attribute to the world at large the opinions of one solitary, ill-informed, and misguided individual.

My first assertion is one that I think you will grant—that every one in this room is a judge of character. Indeed it would be impossible to live for a year without disaster unless one practised character-reading and had some skill in the art. Our marriages, our friendships depend on it; our business largely depends on it; every day questions arise which can only be solved by its help. And now I will hazard a second assertion, which is more disputable perhaps, to the effect that on or about December 1910 human character changed.

I am not saying that one went out, as one might into a garden, and there saw that a rose had flowered, or that a hen had laid an egg. The change was not sudden and definite like that. But a change there was, nevertheless; and, since one must be arbitrary, let us date it about the year 1910. The first signs of it are recorded in the books of Samuel Butler, in The Way of All Flesh in particular; the plays of Bernard Shaw continue to record it. In life one can see the change, if I may use a homely illustration, in the character of one's cook. The Victorian cook lived like a leviathan in the lower depths, formidable, silent, obscure, inscrutable; the Georgian cook is a creature of sunshine and fresh air; in and out of the drawing-room, now to borrow The Daily Herald, now to ask advice about a hat. Do you ask for more solemn instances of the power of the human race to change? Read the gamemnon, and see whether, in process of time, your sympathies are not almost entirely with Clytemnestra. Or consider the married life of the Carlyles, and bewail the waste, the futility, for him and for her, of the horrible domestic tradition which made it seemly for a woman of genius to spend her time chasing beetles, scouring saucepans, instead of writing books. All human relations have shifted—those between masters and servants, husbands and wives, parents and children. And when human relations change there is at the same time a change in religion, conduct, politics, and literature. Let us agree to place one of these changes about the year 1910.

I have said that people have to acquire a good deal of skill in character-reading if they are to live a single year of life without disaster. But it is the art of the young. In middle age and in old age the art is practised mostly for its uses, and friendships and other adventures and experiments in the art of reading character are seldom made. But novelists differ from the rest of the world because they do not cease to be interested in character when they have learnt enough about it for practical purposes. They go a step further; they feel that there is something permanently interesting in character in itself. When all the practical business of life has been discharged, there is something about people which continues to seem to them of overwhelming importance, in spite of the fact that it has no bearing whatever upon their happiness, comfort, or income. The study of character becomes to them an absorbing pursuit; to impart character an obsession. And this I find it very difficult to explain: what novelists mean when they talk about character, what the impulse is that urges them so powerfully every now



A Haunted House and other writings

and then to embody their view in writing.

So, if you will allow me, instead of analysing and abstracting, I will tell you a simple story which, however pointless, has the merit of being true, of a journey from Richmond to Waterloo, in the hope that I may show you what I mean by character in itself; that you may realise the different aspects it can wear; and the hideous perils that beset you directly you try to describe it in words.

One night some weeks ago, then, I was late for the train and jumped into the first carriage I came to. As I sat down I had the strange and uncomfortable feeling that I was interrupting a conversation between two people who were already sitting there. Not that they were young or happy. Far from it. They were both elderly, the woman over sixty, the man well over forty. They were sitting opposite each other, and the man, who had been leaning over and talking emphatically to judge by his attitude and the flush on his face, sat back and became silent. I had disturbed him, and he was annoyed. The elderly lady, however, whom I will call Mrs. Brown, seemed rather relieved. She was one of those clean, threadbare old ladies whose extreme tidiness—everything buttoned, fastened, tied together, mended and brushed up—suggests more extreme poverty than rags and dirt. There was something pinched about her—a look of suffering, of apprehension, and, in addition, she was extremely small. Her feet, in their clean little boots, scarcely touched the floor. I felt that she had nobody to support her; that she had to make up her mind for herself; that, having been deserted, or left a widow, years ago, she had led an anxious, harried life, bringing up an only son, perhaps, who, as likely as not, was by this time beginning to go to the bad. All this shot through my mind as I sat down, being uncomfortable, like most people, at travelling with fellow passengers unless I have somehow or other accounted for them. Then I looked at the man. He was no relation of Mrs. Brown's I felt sure; he was of a bigger, burlier, less refined type. He was a man of business

I imagined, very likely a respectable corn-chandler from the North, dressed in good blue serge with a pocket-knife and a silk handkerchief, and a stout leather bag. Obviously, however, he had an unpleasant business to settle with Mrs. Brown; a secret, perhaps sinister business, which they did not intend to discuss in my presence.

"Yes, the Crofts have had very bad luck with their servants," Mr. Smith (as I will call him) said in a considering way, going back to some earlier topic, with a view to keeping up appearances.

"Ah, poor people," said Mrs. Brown, a trifle condescendingly. "My grandmother had a maid who came when she was fifteen and stayed till she was eighty" (this was said with a kind of hurt and aggressive pride to impress us both perhaps).

"One doesn't often come across that sort of thing nowadays," said Mr. Smith in conciliatory tones.

Then they were silent.

"It's odd they don't start a golf club there—I should have thought one of the young fellows would," said Mr. Smith, for the silence obviously made him uneasy.

Mrs. Brown hardly took the trouble to answer.

"What changes they're making in this part of the world," said Mr. Smith looking out of the window, and looking furtively at me as he did do.

It was plain, from Mrs. Brown's silence, from the uneasy affability with which Mr. Smith spoke, that he had some power over her which he was exerting disagreeably. It might have been her son's downfall, or some painful episode in her past life, or her daughter's. Perhaps she was going to London to sign some document to make over some property. Obviously against her will she was in Mr. Smith's hands. I was beginning to feel a great deal of pity for her, when she said, suddenly and inconsequently,

"Can you tell me if an oak-tree dies when the leaves have been eaten for two years in succession by caterpillars?" She spoke quite brightly, and rather precisely, in a cultivated, inquisitive voice.

Mr. Smith was startled, but relieved to have a safe topic of conversation given him. He told her a great deal very quickly about plagues of insects. He told her that he had a brother who kept a fruit farm in Kent. He told her what fruit farmers do every year in Kent, and so on, and so on. While he talked a very odd thing happened. Mrs. Brown took out her little white handkerchief and began to dab her eyes. She was crying. But she went on listening quite composedly to what he was saying, and he went on talking, a little louder, a little angrily, as if he had seen her cry often before; as if it were a painful habit. At last it got on his nerves. He stopped abruptly, looked out of the window, then leant towards her as he had been doing when I got in, and said in a bullying, menacing way, as if he would not stand any more nonsense,

"So about that matter we were discussing. It'll be all right? George will be there on Tuesday?"

"We shan't be late," said Mrs. Brown, gathering herself together with superb dignity.

Mr. Smith said nothing. He got up, buttoned his coat, reached his bag down, and jumped out of the train before it had stopped at Clapham Junction. He had got what he wanted, but he was ashamed of himself; he was glad to get out of the old lady's sight.

Mrs. Brown and I were left alone together. She sat in her corner opposite, very clean, very small, rather queer, and suffering intensely. The impression she made was overwhelming. It came pouring out like a draught, like a smell of burning. What was it composed of—that overwhelming and peculiar impression? Myriads of irrelevant and incongruous ideas crowd into one's head on such occasions; one sees the person, one sees Mrs. Brown, in the centre of all sorts of different scenes. I thought of her in a seaside house, among queer ornaments: sea-urchins, models of ships in glass cases. Her husband's medals were on the mantelpiece. She popped in and out of the room, perching on the edges of chairs, picking meals out of saucers, indulging in long, silent stares. The caterpillars and the oak-trees seemed to imply all that. And then, into this fantastic and secluded life, in broke Mr. Smith. I saw him blowing in, so to speak, on a windy day. He banged, he slammed. His dripping umbrella made a pool in the hall. They sat closeted together.

And then Mrs. Brown faced the dreadful revelation. She took her heroic decision. Early, before dawn, she packed her bag and carried it herself to the station. She would not let Smith touch it. She was wounded in her pride, unmoored from her anchorage; she came of gentlefolks who kept servants— but details could wait. The important thing was to realise her character, to steep oneself in her atmosphere. I had no time to explain why I felt it somewhat tragic, heroic, yet with a dash of the flighty, and fantastic, before the train stopped, and I watched her disappear, carrying her bag, into the vast blazing station. She looked very small, very tenacious; at once very frail and very heroic. And I have never seen her again, and I shall never know what became of her.

The story ends without any point to it. But I have not told you this anecdote to illustrate either my own ingenuity or the pleasure of travelling from Richmond to Waterloo. What I want you to see in it is this. Here is a character imposing itself upon another person. Here is Mrs. Brown making someone begin almost automatically to write a novel about her. I believe that all novels begin with an old lady in the corner opposite. I believe that all novels, that is to say, deal with character, and that it is to express character—not to preach doctrines, sing songs, or celebrate the glories of the British Empire, that the form of the novel, so clumsy, verbose, and undramatic, so rich, elastic, and alive, has been evolved. To express character, I have said; but you will at once reflect that the very widest interpretation can be put upon those words. For example, old Mrs. Brown's character will strike you very differently according to the age and country in which you happen to be born. It would be easy enough to write three different versions of that incident in the train, an English, a French, and a Russian. The English writer would make the old lady into a 'character'; he would bring out her oddities and mannerisms; her buttons and wrinkles; her ribbons and warts. Her personality would dominate the book. A French writer would rub out all that; he would sacrifice the individual Mrs. Brown to give a more general view of human nature; to make a more abstract, proportioned, and harmonious whole. The Russian would pierce through the flesh; would reveal the soul—the soul alone, wandering out into the Waterloo Road, asking of life some tremendous question which would sound on and on in our ears after the book was finished. And then besides age and country there is the writer's temperament to be considered. You see one thing in character, and I another. You say it means this, and I that. And when it comes to writing each makes a further selection on principles of his own. Thus Mrs. Brown can be treated in an infinite variety of ways, according to the age, country, and temperament of the writer.

But now I must recall what Mr. Arnold Bennett says. He says that it is only if the characters are real that the novel has any chance of surviving. Otherwise, die it must. But, I ask myself, what is reality? And who are the judges of reality? A character may be real to Mr. Bennett and quite unreal to me. For instance, in this article he says that Dr. Watson in Sherlock Holmes is real to him: to me Dr. Watson is a sack stuffed with straw, a dummy, a figure of fun. And so it is with character after character—in book after book. There is nothing that people differ about more than the reality of characters, especially in contemporary books. But if you take a larger view I think that Mr. Bennett is perfectly right. If, that is, you think of the novels which seem to you great novels—War and Peace, Vanity Fair, Tristram Shandy, Madame Bovary, Pride and Prejudice, The Mayor of Casterbridge, Villette—if you think of these books, you do at once think of some character who has seemed to you so real (I do not by that mean so lifelike) that it has the power to make you think not merely of it itself, but of all sorts of things through its eyes—of religion, of love, of war, of peace, of family life, of balls in county towns, of sunsets, moonrises, the immortality of the soul. There is hardly any subject of human experience that is left out of War and Peace it seems to me. And in all these novels all these great novelists have brought us to see whatever they wish us to see through some character. Otherwise, they would not be novelists; but poets, historians, or pamphleteers.

But now let us examine what Mr. Bennett went on to say— he said that there was no great novelist among the Georgian writers because they cannot create characters who are real, true, and convincing. And there I cannot agree. There are reasons, excuses, possibilities which I think put a different colour upon the case. It seems so to me at least, but I am well aware that this is a matter about which I am likely to be prejudiced, sanguine, and near-sighted. I will put my view before you in the hope that you will make it impartial, judicial, and broad-minded. Why, then, is it so hard for novelists at present to create characters which seem real, not only to Mr. Bennett, but to the world at large? Why, when October comes round, do the publishers always fail to supply us with a masterpiece?

Surely one reason is that the men and women who began writing novels in 1910 or thereabouts had this great difficulty to face—that there was no English novelist living from whom they could learn their business. Mr. Conrad is a Pole; which sets him apart, and makes him, however admirable, not very helpful. Mr. Hardy has written no novel since 1895. The most prominent and successful novelists in the year 1910 were, I suppose, Mr. Wells, Mr. Bennett, and Mr. Galsworthy. Now it seems to me that to go to these men and ask them to teach you how to write a novel—how to create characters that are real—is precisely like going to a bootmaker and asking him to teach you how to make a watch. Do not let me give you the impression that I do not admire and enjoy their books. They seem to me of great value, and indeed of great necessity. There are seasons when it is more important to have boots than to have watches. To drop metaphor, I think that after the creative activity of the Victorian age it was quite necessary, not only for literature but for life, that someone should write the books that Mr. Wells, Mr. Bennett, and Mr. Galsworthy have written. Yet what odd books they are! Sometimes I wonder if we are right to call them books at all. For they leave one with so strange a feeling of incompleteness and dissatisfaction. In order to complete them it seems necessary to do something—to join a society, or, more desperately, to write a cheque. That done, the restlessness is laid, the book finished; it can be put upon the shelf, and need never be read again. But with the work of other novelists it is different. Tristram Shandy or Pride and Prejudice is complete in itself; it is self-contained; it leaves one with no desire to do anything, except indeed to read the book again, and to understand it better. The difference perhaps is that both Sterne and Jane Austen were interested in things in themselves; in character in itself; in the book in itself. Therefore everything was inside the book, nothing outside. But the Edwardians were never interested in character in itself; or in the book in itself. They were interested in something outside. Their books, then, were incomplete as books, and required that the reader should finish them, actively and practically, for himself.

Perhaps we can make this clearer if we take the liberty of imagining a little party in the railway carriage—Mr. Wells, Mr.

Galsworthy, Mr. Bennett are travelling to Waterloo with Mrs. Brown. Mrs. Brown, I have said, was poorly dressed and very small. She had an anxious, harassed look. I doubt whether she was what you call an educated woman. Seizing upon all these symptoms of the unsatisfactory condition of our primary schools with a rapidity to which I can do no justice, Mr. Wells would instantly project upon the windowpane a vision of a better, breezier, jollier, happier, more adventurous and gallant world, where these musty railway carriages and fusty old women do not exist; where miraculous barges bring tropical fruit to Camberwell by eight o'clock in the morning; where there are public nurseries, fountains, and libraries, dining-rooms, drawing-rooms, and marriages; where every citizen is generous and candid, manly and magnificent, and rather like Mr. Wells himself. But nobody is in the least like Mrs. Brown. There are no Mrs. Browns in Utopia. Indeed I do not think that Mr. Wells, in his passion to make her what she ought to be, would waste a thought upon her as she is. And what would Mr. Galsworthy see? Can we doubt that the walls of Doulton's factory would take his fancy? There are women in that factory who make twenty-five dozen earthenware pots every day. There are mothers in the Mile End Road who depend upon the farthings which those women earn. But there are employers in Surrey who are even now smoking rich cigars while the nightingale sings. Burning with indignation, stuffed with information, arraigning civilisation, Mr. Galsworthy would only see in Mrs. Brown a pot broken on the wheel and thrown into the corner.

Mr. Bennett, alone of the Edwardians, would keep his eyes in the carriage. He, indeed, would observe every detail with immense care. He would notice the advertisements; the pictures of Swanage and Portsmouth; the way in which the cushion bulged between the buttons; how Mrs. Brown wore a brooch which had cost three-and-ten-three at Whitworth's bazaar; and had mended both gloves—indeed the thumb of the left-hand glove had been replaced. And he would observe, at length, how this was the non-stop train from Windsor which calls at Richmond for the convenience of middle-class residents, who can afford to go to the theatre but have not reached the social rank which can afford motor-cars, though it is true, there are occasions (he would tell us what), when they hire them from a company (he would tell us which). And so he would gradually sidle sedately towards Mrs. Brown, and would remark how she had been left a little copyhold, not freehold, property at Datchet, which, however, was mortgaged to Mr. Bungay the solicitor—but why should. I presume to invent Mr. Bennett? Does not Mr. Bennett write novels himself? I will open the first book that chance puts in my way—Hilda Lessways. Let us see how he makes us feel that Hilda is real, true, and convincing, as a novelist should. She shut the door in a soft, controlled way, which showed the constraint of her relations with her mother. She was fond of reading Maud; she was endowed with the power to feel intensely. So far, so good; in his leisurely, surefooted way Mr. Bennett is trying in these first pages, where every touch is important, to show us the kind of girl she was.

But then he begins to describe, not Hilda Lessways, but the view from her bedroom window, the excuse being that Mr. Skellorn, the man who collects rents, is coming along that way. Mr. Bennett proceeds:

"The bailiwick of Turnhill lay behind her; and all the murky district of the Five Towns, of which Turnhill is the northern outpost, lay to the south. At the foot of Chatterley Wood the canal wound in large curves on its way towards the undefiled plains of Cheshire and the sea. On the canal-side, exactly opposite to Hilda's window, was a flour-mill, that sometimes made nearly as much smoke as the kilns and the chimneys closing the prospect on either hand. From the flour-mill a bricked path, which separated a considerable row of new cottages from their appurtenant gardens, led straight into Lessways Street, in front of Mrs. Lessways' house. By this path

Mr. Skellorn should have arrived, for he inhabited the farthest of the cottages."

One line of insight would have done more than all those lines of description; but let them pass as the necessary drudgery of the novelist. And now—where is Hilda? Alas. Hilda is still looking out of the window. Passionate and dissatisfied as she was, she was a girl with an eye for houses. She often compared this old Mr. Skellorn with the villas she saw from her bedroom window. Therefore the villas must be described. Mr. Bennett proceeds:

"The row was called Freehold Villas: a consciously proud name in a district where much of the land was copyhold and could only change owners subject to the payment of 'fines,' and to the feudal consent of a 'court' presided over by the agent of a lord of the manor. Most of the dwellings were owned by their occupiers, who, each an absolute monarch of the soil, niggled in his sooty garden of an evening amid the flutter of drying shirts and towels. Freehold Villas symbolised the final triumph of Victorian economics, the apotheosis of the prudent and industrious artisan. It corresponded with a Building Society Secretary's dream of paradise. And indeed it was a very real achievement. Nevertheless, Hilda's irrational contempt would not admit this."

Heaven be praised, we cry! At last we are coming to Hilda herself. But not so fast. Hilda may have been this, that, and the other; but Hilda not only looked at houses, and thought of houses; Hilda lived in a house. And what sort of a house did Hilda live in? Mr. Bennett proceeds:

"It was one of the two middle houses of a detached terrace of four houses built by her grandfather Lessways, the teapot manufacturer; it was the chief of the four, obviously the habitation of the proprietor of the terrace. One of the corner houses comprised a grocer's shop, and this house had been robbed of its just proportion of garden so that the seigneurial garden-plot might be triflingly larger than the other. The terrace was not a terrace of cottages, but of houses rated at from twenty-six to thirty-six pounds a year; beyond the means of artisans and petty insurance agents and rent-collectors. And further, it was well built, generously built; and its architecture, though debased, showed some faint traces of Georgian amenity. It was admittedly the best row of houses in that newly settled quarter of the town. In coming to it out of Freehold Villas Mr. Skellorn obviously came to something superior, wider, more liberal. Suddenly Hilda heard her mother's voice. . . ."

But we cannot hear her mother's voice, or Hilda's voice; we can only hear Mr. Bennett's voice telling us facts about rents and freeholds and copyholds and fines. What can Mr. Bennett be about? I have formed my own opinion of what Mr. Bennett is about—he is trying to make us imagine for him; he is trying to hypnotise us into the belief that, because he has made a house, there must be a person living there. With all his powers of observation, which are marvellous, with all his sympathy and humanity, which are great, Mr. Bennett has never once looked at Mrs. Brown in her corner. There she sits in the corner of the carriage—that carriage which is travelling, not from Richmond to Waterloo, but from one age of English literature to the next, for Mrs. Brown is eternal, Mrs. Brown is human nature, Mrs. Brown changes only on the surface, it is the novelists who get in and out—there she sits and not one of the Edwardian writers has so much as looked at her. They have looked very powerfully, searchingly, and sympathetically out of the window; at factories, at Utopias, even at the decoration and upholstery of the carriage; but never at her, never at life, never at human nature. And so they have developed a technique of novel-writing which suits their purpose; they have made tools and established conventions which do their business. But those tools are not our tools, and that business is not our business. For us those conventions are ruin, those tools are death.

You may well complain of the vagueness of my language.

What is a convention, a tool, you may ask, and what do you mean by saying that Mr. Bennett's and Mr. Wells's and Mr. Galsworthy's conventions are the 'wrong conventions for the Georgian's? The question is difficult: I will attempt a short cut. A convention in writing is not much different from a convention in manners. Both in life and in literature it is necessary to have some means of bridging the gulf between the hostess and her unknown guest on the one hand, the writer and his unknown reader on the other. The hostess bethinks her of the weather, for generations of hostesses have established the fact that this is a subject of universal interest in which we all believe. She begins by saying that we are having a wretched May, and, having thus got into touch with her unknown guest, proceeds to matters of greater interest. So it is in literature. The writer must get into touch with his reader by putting before him something which he recognises, which therefore stimulates his imagination, and makes him willing to co-operate in the far more difficult business of intimacy. And it is of the highest importance that this common meeting-place should be reached easily, almost instinctively, in the dark, with one's eyes shut. Here is Mr. Bennett making use of this common ground in the passage which I have quoted. The problem before him was to make us believe in the reality of Hilda Lessways. So he began, being an Edwardian, by describing accurately and minutely the sort of house Hilda lived in, and the sort of house she saw from the window. House property was the common ground from which the Edwardians found it easy to proceed to intimacy. Indirect as it seems to us, the convention worked admirably, and thousands of Hilda Lessways were launched upon the world by this means. For that age and generation, the convention was a good one.

But now, if you will allow me to pull my own anecdote to pieces, you will see how keenly I felt the lack of a convention, and how serious a matter it is when the tools of one generation are useless for the next. The incident had made a great

   A Haunted House and other writings

impression on me. But how was I to transmit it to you? All I could do was to report as accurately as I could what was said, to describe in detail what was worn, to say, despairingly, that all sorts of scenes rushed into my mind, to proceed to tumble them out pell-mell, and to describe this vivid, this overmastering impression by likening it to a draught or a smell of burning. To tell you the truth, I was also strongly tempted to manufacture a three-volume novel about the old lady's son, and his adventures crossing the Atlantic, and her daughter, and how she kept a milliner's shop in Westminster, the past life of Smith himself, and his house at Sheffield, though such stories seem to me the most dreary, irrelevant, and humbugging affairs in the world.

But if I had done that I should have escaped the appalling effort of saying what I meant. And to have got at what I meant I should have had to go back and back and back; to experiment with one thing and another; to try this sentence and that, referring each word to my vision, matching it as exactly as possible, and knowing that somehow I had to find a common ground between us, a convention which would not seem to you too odd, unreal, and far-fetched to believe in. I admit that I shirked that arduous undertaking. I let my Mrs. Brown slip through my fingers. I have told you nothing whatever about her. But that is partly the great Edwardians' fault. I asked them—they are my elders and betters—How shall I begin to describe this woman's character? And they said, "Begin by saying that her father kept a shop in Harrogate. Ascertain the rent. Ascertain the wages of shop assistants in the year 1878. Discover what her mother died of. Describe cancer. Describe calico. Describe——" But I cried, "Stop! Stop!" And I regret to say that I threw that ugly, that clumsy, that incongruous tool out of the window, for I knew that if I began describing the cancer and the calico, my Mrs. Brown, that vision to which I cling though I know no way of imparting it to you, would have been dulled and tarnished and vanished for ever.

That is what I mean by saying that the Edwardian tools are the wrong ones for us to use. They have laid an enormous stress upon the fabric of things. They have given us a house in the hope that we may be able to deduce the human beings who live there. To give them their due, they have made that house much better worth living in. But if you hold that novels are in the first place about people, and only in the second about the houses they live in, that is the wrong way to set about it. Therefore, you see, the Georgian writer had to begin by throwing away the method that was in use at the moment. He was left alone there facing Mrs. Brown without any method of conveying her to the reader. But that is inaccurate. A writer is never alone. There is always the public with him—if not on the same seat, at least in the compartment next door. Now the public is a strange travelling companion. In England it is a very suggestible and docile creature, which, once you get it to attend, will believe implicitly what it is told for a certain number of years. If you say to the public with sufficient conviction, "All women have tails, and all men humps," it will actually learn to see women with tails and men with humps, and will think it very revolutionary and probably improper if you say "Nonsense. Monkeys have tails and camels humps. But men and women have brains, and they have hearts; they think and they feel,"—that will seem to it a bad joke, and an improper one into the bargain.

But to return. Here is the British public sitting by the writer's side and saying in its vast and unanimous way, "Old women have houses. They have fathers. They have incomes. They have servants. They have hot water bottles. That is how we know that they are old women. Mr. Wells and Mr. Bennett and Mr. Galsworthy have always taught us that this is the way to recognise them. But now with your Mrs. Brown—how are we to believe in her? We do not even know whether her villa was called Albert or Balmoral; what she paid for her gloves; or whether her mother died of cancer or of consumption.

   

How can she be alive? No; she is a mere figment of your imagination."

And old women of course ought to be made of freehold villas and copyhold estates, not of imagination.

The Georgian novelist, therefore, was in an awkward predicament. There was Mrs. Brown protesting that she was different, quite different, from what people made out, and luring the novelist to her rescue by the most fascinating if fleeting glimpse of her charms; there were the Edwardians handing out tools appropriate to house building and house breaking; and there was the British public asseverating that they must see the hot water bottle first. Meanwhile the train was rushing to that station where we must all get out.

Such, I think, was the predicament in which the young Georgians found themselves about the year 1910. Many of them—I am thinking of Mr. Forster and Mr. Lawrence in particular—spoilt their early work because, instead of throwing away those tools, they tried to use them. They tried to compromise. They tried to combine their own direct sense of the oddity and significance of some character with Mr. Galsworthy's knowledge of the Factory Acts, and Mr. Bennett's knowledge of the Five Towns. They tried it, but they had too keen, too overpowering a sense of Mrs. Brown and her peculiarities to go on trying it much longer. Something had to be done. At whatever cost of life, limb, and damage to valuable property Mrs. Brown must be rescued, expressed, and set in her high relations to the world before the train stopped and she disappeared for ever. And so the smashing and the crashing began. Thus it is that we hear all round us, in poems and novels and biographies, even in newspaper articles and essays, the sound of breaking and falling, crashing and destruction. It is the prevailing sound of the Georgian age—rather a melancholy one if you think what melodious days there have been in the past, if you think of Shakespeare and Milton and Keats or even of Jane Austen and Thackeray and Dickens; if you think of the language, and the heights to which it can soar when free, and see the same eagle captive, bald, and croaking.

In view of these facts—with these sounds in my ears and these fancies in my brain—I am not going to deny that Mr. Bennett has some reason when he complains that our Georgian writers are unable to make us believe that our characters are real. I am forced to agree that they do not pour out three immortal masterpieces with Victorian regularity every autumn. But instead of being gloomy, I am sanguine. For this state of things is, I think, inevitable whenever from hoar old age or callow youth the convention ceases to be a means of communication between writer and reader, and becomes instead an obstacle and an impediment. At the present moment we are suffering, not from decay, but from having no code of manners which writers and readers accept as a prelude to the more exciting intercourse of friendship. The literary convention of the time is so artificial—you have to talk about the weather and nothing but the weather throughout the entire visit—that, naturally, the feeble are tempted to outrage, and the strong are led to destroy the very foundations and rules of literary society. Signs of this are everywhere apparent. Grammar is violated; syntax disintegrated; as a boy staying with an aunt for the weekend rolls in the geranium bed out of sheer desperation as the solemnities of the sabbath wear on. The more adult writers do not, of course, indulge in such wanton exhibitions of spleen. Their sincerity is desperate, and their courage tremendous; it is only that they do not know which to use, a fork or their fingers. Thus, if you read Mr. Joyce and Mr. Eliot you will be struck by the indecency of the one, and the obscurity of the other. Mr. Joyce's indecency in Ulysses seems to me the conscious and calculated indecency of a desperate man who feels that in order to breathe he must break the windows. At moments, when the window is broken, he is magnificent. But what a waste of energy! And, after all, how dull indecency is, when it is not the overflowing of a superabundant energy or savagery, but the determined and public-spirited act of a man who needs fresh air! Again, with the obscurity of Mr. Eliot. I think that Mr. Eliot has written some of the loveliest single lines in modern poetry. But how intolerant he is of the old usages and politenesses of society—respect for the weak, consideration for the dull! As I sun myself upon the intense and ravishing beauty of one of his lines, and reflect that I must make a dizzy and dangerous leap to the next, and so on from line to line, like an acrobat flying precariously from bar to bar, I cry out, I confess, for the old decorums, and envy the indolence of my ancestors who, instead of spinning madly through mid-air, dreamt quietly in the shade with a book. Again, in Mr. Strachey's books, "Eminent Victorians" and "Queen Victoria," the effort and strain of writing against the grain and current of the times is visible too. It is much less visible, of course, for not only is he dealing with facts, which are stubborn things, but he has fabricated, chiefly from eighteenth-century material, a very discreet code of manners of his own, which allows him to sit at table with the highest in the land and to say a great many things under cover of that exquisite apparel which, had they gone naked, would have been chased by the men-servants from the room. Still, if you compare "Eminent Victorians" with some of Lord Macaulay's essays, though you will feel that Lord Macaulay is always wrong, and Mr. Strachey always right, you will also feel a body, a sweep, a richness in Lord Macaulay's essays which show that his age was behind him; all his strength went straight into his work; none was used for purposes of concealment or of conversion. But Mr. Strachey has had to open our eyes before he made us see; he has had to search out and sew together a very artful manner of speech; and the effort, beautifully though it is concealed, has robbed his work of some of the force that should have gone into it, and limited his scope.

For these reasons, then, we must reconcile ourselves to a

season of failures and fragments. We must reflect that where so much strength is spent on finding a way of telling the truth the truth itself is bound to reach us in rather an exhausted and chaotic condition. Ulysses, Queen Victoria, Mr. Prufrock—to give Mrs. Brown some of the names she has made famous lately—is a little pale and dishevelled by the time her rescuers reach her. And it is the sound of their axes that we hear—a vigorous and stimulating sound in my ears—unless of course you wish to sleep, when, in the bounty of his concern. Providence has provided a host of writers anxious and able to satisfy your needs.

Thus I have tried, at tedious length, I fear, to answer some of the questions which I began by asking. I have given an account of some of the difficulties which in my view beset the Georgian writer in all his forms. I have sought to excuse him. May I end by venturing to remind you of the duties and responsibilities that are yours as partners in this business of writing books, as companions in the railway carriage, as fellow travellers with Mrs. Brown? For she is just as visible to you who remain silent as to us who tell stories about her. In the course of your daily life this past week you have had far stranger and more interesting experiences than the one I have tried to describe. You have overheard scraps of talk that filled you with amazement. You have gone to bed at night bewildered by the complexity of your feelings. In one day thousands of ideas have coursed through your brains; thousands of emotions have met, collided, and disappeared in astonishing disorder. Nevertheless, you allow the writers to palm off upon you a version of all this, an image of Mrs. Brown, which has no likeness to that surprising apparition whatsoever. In your modesty you seem to consider that writers are of different blood and bone from yourselves; that they know more of Mrs. Brown than you do. Never was there a more fatal mistake. It is this division between reader and writer, this humility on your part, these professional airs and graces on ours, that corrupt and emasculate the books

                    A Haunted House and other writings

which should be the healthy offspring of a close and equal alliance between us. Hence spring those sleek, smooth novels, those portentous and ridiculous biographies, that milk and watery criticism, those poems melodiously celebrating the innocence of roses and sheep which pass so plausibly for literature at the present time.

Your part is to insist that writers shall come down off their plinths and pedestals, and describe beautifully if possible, truthfully at any rate, our Mrs. Brown. You should insist that she is an old lady of unlimited capacity and infinite variety; capable of appearing in any place; wearing any dress; saying anything and doing heaven knows what. But the things she says and the things she does and her eyes and her nose and her speech and her silence have an overwhelming fascination, for she is, of course, the spirit we live by, life itself.

But do not expect just at present a complete and satisfactory presentment of her. Tolerate the spasmodic, the obscure, the fragmentary, the failure. Your help is invoked in a good cause. For I will make one final and surpassingly rash prediction—we are trembling on the verge of one of the great ages of English literature. But it can only be reached if we are determined never, never to desert Mrs. Brown.

# Mrs. Dalloway in Bond Street

Mrs Dalloway said she would buy the gloves herself.

Big Ben was striking as she stepped out into the street. It was eleven o'clock and the unused hour was fresh as if issued to children on a beach. But there was something solemn in the deliberate swing of the repeated strokes; something stirring in the murmur of wheels and the shuffle of footsteps.

No doubt they were not all bound on errands of happiness. There is much more to be said about us than that we walk the streets of Westminster. Big Ben too is nothing but steel rods consumed by rust were it not for the care of H.M.'s Office of Works. Only for Mrs Dalloway the moment was complete; for Mrs Dalloway June was fresh. A happy childhood--and it was not to his daughters only that Justin Parry had seemed a fine fellow (weak of course on the Bench); flowers at evening, smoke rising; the caw of rooks falling from ever so high, down down through the October air - there is nothing to take the place of childhood. A leaf of mint brings it back: or a cup with a blue ring.

Poor little wretches, she sighed, and pressed forward. Oh, right under the horses' noses, you little demon! and there she was left on the kerb stretching her hand out, while Jimmy Dawes grinned on the further side.

A charming woman, poised, eager, strangely white-haired for her pink cheeks, so Scope Purvis, C.C.B., saw her as he hurried to his office. She stiffened a little, waiting for burthen's van to pass. Big Ben struck the tenth; struck the eleventh stroke. The leaden circles dissolved in the air. Pride held her erect, inheriting, handing on, acquainted with discipline and with suffering. How people suffered, how they suffered, she thought, thinking of Mrs Foxcroft at the Embassy last night decked with jewels, eating her heart out, because that nice boy was dead, and now the old Manor House (Durtnall's van passed) must go to a cousin.

'Good morning to you!' said Hugh Whitbread raising his hat rather extravagantly by the china shop, for they had known each other as children. 'Where are you off to?'

'I love walking in London,' said Mrs Dalloway. 'Really it's better than walking in the country!'

'We've just come up,' said Hugh Whitbread. 'Unfortunately to see doctors.'

'Milly?' said Mrs Dalloway, instantly compassionate.

'Out of sorts,' said Hugh Whitbread. 'That sort of thing. Dick all right?'

'First rate!' said Clarissa.

Of course, she thought, walking on, Milly is about my age--fifty, fifty-two. So it is probably that, Hugh's manner had said so, said it perfectly--dear old Hugh, thought Mrs Dalloway, remembering with amusement, with gratitude, with emotion, how shy, like a brother--one would rather die than speak to one's brother--Hugh had always been, when he was at Oxford, and came over, and perhaps one of them (drat the thing!) couldn't ride. How then could women sit in Parliament? How could they do things with men? For there is this extra-ordinarily deep instinct, something inside one; you can't get over it; it's no use trying; and men like Hugh respect it without our saying it, which is what one loves, thought Clarissa, in dear old Hugh.

She had passed through the Admiralty Arch and saw at the end of the empty road with its thin trees Victoria's white mound, Victoria's billowing motherliness, amplitude and homeliness, always ridiculous, yet how sublime, thought Mrs Dalloway, remembering Kensington Gardens and the old lady in horn spectacles and being told by Nanny to stop dead still and bow to the Queen. The flag flew above the Palace. The King and Queen were back then. Dick had met her at lunch the other day--a thoroughly nice woman. It matters so much to the poor, thought Clarissa, and to the soldiers. A man in bronze stood heroically on a pedestal with a gun on her left hand side--the South African war. It matters, thought Mrs Dalloway walking towards Buckingham Palace. There it stood four-square, in the broad sunshine, uncompromising, plain. But it was character, she thought; something inborn in the race; what Indians respected. The Queen went to hospitals, opened bazaars--the Queen of England, thought Clarissa, looking at the Palace. Already at this hour a motor car passed out at the gates; soldiers saluted; the gates were shut. And Clarissa, crossing the road, entered the Park, holding herself upright.

June had drawn out every leaf on the trees. The mothers of Westminster with mottled breasts gave suck to their young. Quite respectable girls lay stretched on the grass. An elderly man, stooping very stiffly, picked up a crumpled paper, spread it out flat and flung it away. How horrible! Last night at the Embassy Sir Dighton had said, 'If 1 want a fellow to hold my horse, I have only to put up my hand.' But the religious question is far more serious than the economic, Sir Dighton had said, which she thought extraordinarily interesting, from a man like Sir Dighton. 'Oh, the country will never know what it has lost,' he had said, talking of his own accord, about dear Jack Stewart.

She mounted the little hill lightly. The air stirred with energy. Messages were passing from the Fleet to the Admiralty. Piccadilly and Arlington Street and the Mall seemed to chafe the very air in the Park and lift its leaves hotly, brilliantly, upon waves of that divine vitality which Clarissa loved. To ride; to dance; she had adored all that. Or going long walks in the country, talking, about books, what to do with one's life, for young people were amazingly priggish--oh, the things one had said! But one had conviction. Middle age is the devil. People like Jack'll never know that, she thought; for he never once thought of death, never, they said, knew he was dying. And now can never mourn--how did it go?--a head grown grey . . . From the contagion of the world's slow stain, . . . have drunk their cup a round or two before. . . . From the contagion of the world's slow stain! She held herself upright.

But how jack would have shouted! Quoting Shelley, in Piccadilly, 'You want a pin,' he would have said. He hated frumps. 'My God Clarissa! My God Clarissa!'--she could hear him now at the Devonshire House party, about poor Sylvia Hunt in her amber necklace and that dowdy old silk. Clarissa held herself upright for she had spoken aloud and now she was in Piccadilly, passing the house with the slender green columns, and the balconies; passing club windows full of newspapers; passing old Lady Burdett-Coutts' house where the glazed white parrot used to hang; and Devonshire House, without its gilt leopards; and Claridge's, where she must remember Dick wanted her to leave a card on Mrs Jepson or she would be gone. Rich Americans can be very charming. There was St James's Palace; like a child's game with bricks; and now--she had passed Bond Street--she was by Hatchard's book shop. The stream was endless--endless endless. Lords, Ascot, Hurlingham--what was it? What a duck, she thought, looking at the frontispiece of some book of memoirs spread wide in the bow window, Sir Joshua perhaps or Romney; arch, bright, demure; the sort of girl--like her own Elizabeth--the only real sort of girl. And there was that absurd book, Soapy Sponge, which Jim used to quote by the yard; and Shakespeare's Sonnets. She knew them by heart. Phil and she had argued all day about the Dark Lady, and Dick had said straight out at dinner that night that he had never heard of her. Really, she had married him for that! He had never read Shakespeare! There must be some little cheap book she could buy for Milly--Cranford of course! Was there ever anything so enchanting as the cow in petticoats? If only people had that sort of humour, that sort of self-respect now, thought Clarissa, for she remembered the broad pages; the sentences ending; the characters--how one talked about them as if they were real. For all the great things one must go to the past, she thought. From the contagion of the world's slow stain . . . Fear no more the heat o' the sun. . . . And now can never mourn, can never mourn, she repeated, her eyes straying over the window; for it ran in her head; the test of great poetry; the moderns had never written anything one wanted to read about death, she thought; and turned.

Omnibuses joined motor cars; motor cars vans; vans taxicabs, taxicabs motor cars--here was an open motor car with a girl, alone. Up till four, her feet tingling, I know, thought Clarissa, for the girl looked washed out, half asleep, in the corner of the car after the dance. And another car came; and another. No! No! No! Clarissa smiled good-naturedly. The fat lady had taken every sort of trouble, but diamonds! orchids! at this hour of the morning! No! No! No! The excellent policeman would, when the time came, hold up his hand. Another motor car passed. How utterly unattractive! Why should a girl of that age paint black round her eyes? And a young man, with a girl, at this hour, when the country-- The admirable policeman raised his hand and Clarissa acknowledging his sway, taking her time, crossed, walked towards Bond Street; saw the narrow crooked street, the yellow banners; the thick notched telegraph wires stretched across the sky.

A hundred years ago her great-great-grandfather, Seymour Parry, who ran away with Conway's daughter, had walked down Bond Street. Down Bond Street the Parrys had walked for a hundred years, and might have met the Dalloways (Leighs on the mother's side) going up. Her father got his clothes from Hill's. There was a roll of cloth in the window, and here just one jar on a black table, incredibly expensive; like the thick pink salmon on the ice block at the fish monger's. The jewels were exquisite--pink and orange stars, paste, Spanish, she thought, and chains of old gold; starry buckles, little brooches which had been worn on sea-green satin by ladies with high head-dresses. But no good looking! One must economise. She must go on past the picture dealer's where one of the odd French pictures hung, as if people had thrown confetti--pink and blue--for a joke. If you had lived with pictures (and it's the same with books and music) thought Clarissa, passing the Aeolian Hall, you can't be taken in by a joke.

The river of Bond Street was clogged. There, like a Queen at a tournament, raised, regal, was Lady Bexborough. She sat in her carriage, upright, alone, looking through her glasses. The white glove was loose at her wrist. She was in black, quite shabby, yet, thought Clarissa, how extraordinarily it tells, breeding, self-respect, never saying a word too much or letting people gossip; an astonishing friend; no one can pick a hole in her after all these years, and now, there she is, thought Clarissa, passing the Countess who waited powdered, perfectly still, and Clarissa would have given anything to be like that, the mistress of Clarefield, talking politics, like a man. But she never goes anywhere, thought Clarissa, and it's quite useless to ask her, and the carriage went on and Lady Bexborough was borne past like a Queen at a tournament, though she had nothing to live for and the old man is failing and they say she is sick of it all, thought Clarissa and the tears actually rose to her eyes as she entered the shop.

'Good morning,' said Clarissa in her charming voice. 'Gloves,' she said with her exquisite friendliness and putting her bag on the counter began, very slowly, to undo the buttons. 'White gloves,' she said. 'Above the elbow,' and she looked straight into the shop-woman's face--but this was not the girl she remembered? She looked quite old. 'These really don't fit,' said Clarissa. The shop-girl looked at them. 'Madame wears bracelets?' Clarissa spread out her fingers. 'Perhaps it's my rings.' And the girl took the grey gloves with her to the end of the counter.

Yes, thought Clarissa, if it's the girl I remember, she's twenty years older. . .. There was only one other customer, sitting sideways at the counter, her elbow poised, her bare hand drooping, vacant; like a figure on a Japanese fan, thought Clarissa, too vacant perhaps, yet some men would adore her. The lady shook her head sadly. Again the gloves were too large. She turned round the glass. 'Above the wrist,' she reproached the grey-headed woman; who looked and agreed.

They waited; a clock ticked; Bond Street hummed, dulled, distant; the woman went away holding gloves. 'Above the wrist,' said the lady, mournfully, raising her voice. And she would have to order chairs, ices, flowers, and cloak-room tickets, thought Clarissa. The people she didn't want would come; the others wouldn't. She would stand by the door. They sold stockings--silk stockings. A lady is known by her gloves and her shoes, old Uncle William used to say. And through the hanging silk stockings quivering silver she looked at the lady, sloping shouldered, her hand drooping, her bag slipping, her eyes vacantly on the floor. It would be intolerable if dowdy women came to her party! Would one have liked Keats if he had worn red socks? Oh, at last--she drew into the counter and it flashed into her mind:

'Do you remember before the war you had gloves with pearl buttons?'

'French gloves, Madame?'

'Yes, they were French,' said Clarissa. The other lady rose very sadly and took her bag, and looked at the gloves on the counter. But they were all too large--always too large at the wrist.

'With pearl buttons,' said the shop-girl, who looked ever so much older. She split the lengths of tissue paper apart on the counter. With pearl buttons, thought Clarissa, perfectly simple--how French!

                    A Haunted House and other writings

'Madame's hands are so slender,' said the shop-girl, drawing the glove firmly, smoothly, down over her rings. And Clarissa looked at her arm in the looking-glass. The glove hardly came to the elbow. Were there others half an inch longer? Still it seemed tiresome to bother her perhaps the one day in the month, thought Clarissa, when it's an agony to stand. 'Oh, don't bother,' she said. But the gloves were brought.

'Don't you get fearfully tired,' she said in her charming voice, 'standing? When d'you get your holiday?'

'In September, Madame, when we're not so busy.'

When we're in the country thought Clarissa. Or shooting. She has a fortnight at Brighton. In some stuffy lodging. The landlady takes the sugar. Nothing would be easier than to send her to Mrs Lumley's right in the country (and it was on the tip of her tongue). But then she remembered how on their honeymoon Dick had shown her the folly of giving impulsively. It was much more important, he said, to get trade with China. Of course he was right. And she could feel the girl wouldn't like to be given things. There she was in her place. So was Dick. Selling gloves was her job. She had her own sorrows quite separate, 'and now can never mourn, can never mourn,' the words ran in her head. 'From the contagion of the world's slow stain,' thought Clarissa holding her arm stiff, for there are moments when it seems utterly futile (the glove was drawn off leaving her arm flecked with powder)--simply one doesn't believe, thought Clarissa, any more in God.

The traffic suddenly roared; the silk stockings brightened. A customer came in.

'White gloves,' she said, with some ring in her voice that Clarissa remembered.

It used, thought Clarissa, to be so simple. Down down through the air came the caw of the rooks. When Sylvia died, hundreds of years ago, the yew hedges looked so lovely with the diamond webs in the mist before early church. But if Dick were to die tomorrow, as for believing in God--no, she would let the children choose, but for herself, like Lady Bexborough, who opened the bazaar, they say, with the telegram in her hand--Roden, her favourite, killed--she would go on. But why, if one doesn't believe? For the sake of others, she thought, taking the glove in her hand. The girl would be much more unhappy if she didn't believe.

'Thirty shillings,' said the shop-woman. 'No, pardon me Madame, thirty-five. The French gloves are more.'

For one doesn't live for oneself, thought Clarissa.

And then the other customer took a glove, tugged it, and it split.

'There!' she exclaimed .

'A fault of the skin,' said the grey-headed woman hurriedly. 'Sometimes a drop of acid in tanning. Try this pair, Madame.'

'But it's an awful swindle to ask two pound ten!'

Clarissa looked at the lady; the lady looked at Clarissa.

'Gloves have never been quite so reliable since the war,' said the shop-girl, apologising, to Clarissa.

But where had she seen the other lady?--elderly, with a frill under her chin; wearing a black ribbon for gold eyeglasses; sensual, clever, like a Sargent drawing. How one can tell from a voice when people are in the habit, thought Clarissa, of making other people--'It's a shade too tight,' she said--obey. The shop-woman went off again. Clarissa was left waiting. Fear no more she repeated, playing her finger on the counter. Fear no more the heat o' the sun. Fear no more she repeated. There were little brown spots on her arm. And the girl crawled like a snail. Thou thy worldly task hast done. Thousands of young men had died that things might go on. At last! Half an rich above the elbow;

                    

pearl buttons; five and a quarter. My dear slow coach, thought Clarissa, do you think I can sit here the whole morning? Now you'll take twenty-five minutes to bring me my change!

There was a violent explosion in the street outside. The shop-women cowered behind the counters. But Clarissa, sitting very upright, smiled at the other lady. 'Miss Anstruther!' she exclaimed.

# The Mark On The Wall

PERHAPS IT WAS the middle of January in the present year that I first looked up and saw the mark on the wall. In order to fix a date it is necessary to remember what one saw. So now I think of the fire; the steady film of yellow light upon the page of my book; the three chrysanthemums in the round glass bowl on the mantelpiece. Yes, it must have been the winter time, and we had just finished our tea, for I remember that I was smoking a cigarette when I looked up and saw the mark on the wall for the first time. I looked up through the smoke of my cigarette and my eye lodged for a moment upon the burning coals, and that old fancy of the crimson flag flapping from the castle tower came into my mind, and I thought of the cavalcade of red knights riding up the side of the black rock. Rather to my relief the sight of the mark interrupted the fancy, for it is an old fancy, an automatic fancy, made as a child perhaps. The mark was a small round mark, black upon the white wall, about six or seven inches above the mantelpiece.

How readily our thoughts swarm upon a new object, lifting it a little way, as ants carry a blade of straw so feverishly, and then leave it.... If that mark was made by a nail, it can't have been for a picture, it must have been for a miniaturethe miniature of a lady with white powdered curls, powder-dusted cheeks, and lips like red carnations. A fraud of course, for the people who had this house before us would have chosen pictures in that wayan old picture for an old room. That is the sort of people they werevery interesting people, and I think of them so often, in such queer places, because one will never see them again, never know what happened next. They wanted to leave this house because they wanted to change their style of furniture, so he said, and he was in process of saying that in his opinion art should have ideas behind it when we were torn asunder, as one is torn from the old lady about to pour out tea and the young man about to hit the tennis ball in the back garden of the suburban villa as one rushes past in the train.

But as for that mark, I'm not sure about it; I don't believe it was made by a nail after all; it's too big, too round, for that. I might get up, but if I got up and looked at it, ten to one I shouldn't be able to say for certain; because once a thing's done, no one ever knows how it happened. Oh! dear me, the mystery of life; The inaccuracy of thought! The ignorance of humanity! To show how very little control of our possessions we havewhat an accidental affair this living is after all our civilizationlet me just count over a few of the things lost in one lifetime, beginning, for that seems always the most mysterious of losseswhat cat would gnaw, what rat would nibblethree pale blue canisters of book-binding tools? Then there were the bird cages, the iron hoops, the steel skates, the Queen Anne coal-scuttle, the bagatelle board, the hand organall gone, and jewels, too. Opals and emeralds, they lie about the roots of turnips. What a scraping paring affair it is to be sure! The wonder is that I've any clothes on my back, that I sit surrounded by solid furniture at this moment. Why, if one wants to compare life to anything, one must liken it to being blown through the Tube at fifty miles an hourlanding at the other end without a single hairpin in one's hair! Shot out at the feet of God entirely naked! Tumbling head over heels in the asphodel meadows like brown paper parcels pitched down a shoot in the post office! With one's hair flying back like the tail of a race-horse. Yes, that seems to express the rapidity of life, the perpetual waste and repair; all so casual, all so haphazard....

But after life. The slow pulling down of thick green stalks so that the cup of the flower, as it turns over, deluges one with purple and red light. Why, after all, should one not be born there as one is born here, helpless, speechless, unable to focus one's eyesight, groping at the roots of the grass, at the toes of the Giants? As for saying which are trees, and which are men and women, or whether there are such things, that one won't be in a condition to do for fifty years or so. There will be nothing but spaces of light and dark, intersected by thick stalks, and rather higher up perhaps, rose-shaped blots of an indistinct colourdim pinks and blueswhich will, as time goes on, become more definite, becomeI don't know what....

And yet that mark on the wall is not a hole at all. It may even be caused by some round black substance, such as a small rose leaf, left over from the summer, and I, not being a very vigilant housekeeperlook at the dust on the mantelpiece, for example, the dust which, so they say, buried Troy three times over, only fragments of pots utterly refusing annihilation, as one can believe.

The tree outside the window taps very gently on the pane.... I want to think quietly, calmly, spaciously, never to be interrupted, never to have to rise from my chair, to slip easily from one thing to another, without any sense of hostility, or obstacle. I want to sink deeper and deeper, away from the surface, with its hard separate facts. To steady myself, let me catch hold of the first idea that passes.... Shakespeare.... Well, he will do as well as another. A man who sat himself solidly in an arm-chair, and looked into the fire, soA shower of ideas fell perpetually from some very high Heaven down through his mind. He leant his forehead on his hand, and people, looking in through the open door,for this scene is supposed to take place on a summer's eveningBut how dull this is, this historical fiction! It doesn't interest me at all. I wish I could hit upon a pleasant track of thought, a track indirectly reflecting credit upon myself, for those are the pleasantest thoughts, and very frequent even in the minds of modest mouse-coloured people, who believe genuinely that they dislike to hear their own praises. They are not thoughts directly praising oneself; that is the beauty of them; they are thoughts like this:

"And then I came into the room. They were discussing

     A Haunted House and other writings

botany. I said how I'd seen a flower growing on a dust heap on the site of an old house in Kingsway. The seed, I said, must have been sown in the reign of Charles the First. What flowers grew in the reign of Charles the First?" I asked(but I don't remember the answer). Tall flowers with purple tassels to them perhaps. And so it goes on. All the time I'm dressing up the figure of myself in my own mind, lovingly, stealthily, not openly adoring it, for if I did that, I should catch myself out, and stretch my hand at once for a book in self-protection. Indeed, it is curious how instinctively one protects the image of oneself from idolatry or any other handling that could make it ridiculous, or too unlike the original to be believed in any longer. Or is it not so very curious after all? It is a matter of great importance. Suppose the looking glass smashes, the image disappears, and the romantic figure with the green of forest depths all about it is there no longer, but only that shell of a person which is seen by other peoplewhat an airless, shallow, bald, prominent world it becomes! A world not to be lived in. As we face each other in omnibuses and underground railways we are looking into the mirror; that accounts for the vagueness, the gleam of glassiness, in our eyes. And the novelists in future will realize more and more the importance of these reflections, for of course there is not one reflection but an almost infinite number; those are the depths they will explore, those the phantoms they will pursue, leaving the description of reality more and more out of their stories, taking a knowledge of it for granted, as the Greeks did and Shakespeare perhapsbut these generalizations are very worthless. The military sound of the word is enough. It recalls leading articles, cabinet ministersa whole class of things indeed which as a child one thought the thing itself, the standard thing, the real thing, from which one could not depart save at the risk of nameless damnation. Generalizations bring back somehow Sunday in London, Sunday afternoon walks, Sunday luncheons, and also ways of speaking of the dead, clothes, and habitslike the habit of sitting all together in one room until a certain hour, although nobody liked it. There was a rule for everything. The rule for tablecloths at that particular period was that they should be made of tapestry with little yellow compartments marked upon them, such as you may see in photographs of the carpets in the corridors of the royal palaces. Tablecloths of a different kind were not real tablecloths. How shocking, and yet how wonderful it was to discover that these real things, Sunday luncheons, Sunday walks, country houses, and tablecloths were not entirely real, were indeed half phantoms, and the damnation which visited the disbeliever in them was only a sense of illegitimate freedom. What now takes the place of those things I wonder, those real standard things? Men perhaps, should you be a woman; the masculine point of view which governs our lives, which sets the standard, which establishes Whitaker's Table of Precedency, which has become, I suppose, since the war half a phantom to many men and women, which soon, one may hope, will be laughed into the dustbin where the phantoms go, the mahogany sideboards and the Landseer prints, Gods and Devils, Hell and so forth, leaving us all with an intoxicating sense of illegitimate freedomif freedom exists....

In certain lights that mark on the wall seems actually to project from the wall. Nor is it entirely circular. I cannot be sure, but it seems to cast a perceptible shadow, suggesting that if I ran my finger down that strip of the wall it would, at a certain point, mount and descend a small tumulus, a smooth tumulus like those barrows on the South Downs which are, they say, either tombs or camps. Of the two I should prefer them to be tombs, desiring melancholy like most English people, and finding it natural at the end of a walk to think of the bones stretched beneath the turf.... There must be some book about it. Some antiquary must have dug up those bones and given them a name.... What sort of a man is an antiquary, I wonder? Retired Colonels for the most part, I daresay, leading parties of aged labourers to the top here, examining clods of

 A Haunted House and other writings

earth and stone, and getting into correspondence with the neighbouring clergy, which, being opened at breakfast time, gives them a feeling of importance, and the comparison of arrow-heads necessitates cross-country journeys to the county towns, an agreeable necessity both to them and to their elderly wives, who wish to make plum jam or to clean out the study, and have every reason for keeping that great question of the camp or the tomb in perpetual suspension, while the Colonel himself feels agreeably philosophic in accumulating evidence on both sides of the question. It is true that he does finally incline to believe in the camp; and, being opposed, indites a pamphlet which he is about to read at the quarterly meeting of the local society when a stroke lays him low, and his last conscious thoughts are not of wife or child, but of the camp and that arrowhead there, which is now in the case at the local museum, together with the foot of a Chinese murderess, a handful of Elizabethan nails, a great many Tudor clay pipes, a piece of Roman pottery, and the wine-glass that Nelson drank out ofproving I really don't know what.

No, no, nothing is proved, nothing is known. And if I were to get up at this very moment and ascertain that the mark on the wall is reallywhat shall we say?the head of a gigantic old nail, driven in two hundred years ago, which has now, owing to the patient attrition of many generations of housemaids, revealed its head above the coat of paint, and is taking its first view of modern life in the sight of a white-walled fire-lit room, what should I gain?Knowledge? Matter for further speculation? I can think sitting still as well as standing up. And what is knowledge? What are our learned men save the descendants of witches and hermits who crouched in caves and in woods brewing herbs, interrogating shrew-mice and writing down the language of the stars? And the less we honour them as our superstitions dwindle and our respect for beauty and health of mind increases.... Yes, one could imagine a very pleasant world. A quiet, spacious world, with the flowers so red and blue in the open fields. A world without professors or specialists or house-keepers with the profiles of policemen, a world which one could slice with one's thought as a fish slices the water with his fin, grazing the stems of the water-lilies, hanging suspended over nests of white sea eggs.... How peaceful it is down here, rooted in the centre of the world and gazing up through the grey waters, with their sudden gleams of light, and their reflectionsif it were not for Whitaker's Almanackif it were not for the Table of Precedency!

I must jump up and see for myself what that mark on the wall really isa nail, a rose-leaf, a crack in the wood?

Here is nature once more at her old game of self-preservation. This train of thought, she perceives, is threatening mere waste of energy, even some collision with reality, for who will ever be able to lift a finger against Whitaker's Table of Precedency? The Archbishop of Canterbury is followed by the Lord High Chancellor; the Lord High Chancellor is followed by the Archbishop of York. Everybody follows somebody, such is the philosophy of Whitaker; and the great thing is to know who follows whom. Whitaker knows, and let that, so Nature counsels, comfort you, instead of enraging you; and if you can't be comforted, if you must shatter this hour of peace, think of the mark on the wall.

I understand Nature's gameher prompting to take action as a way of ending any thought that threatens to excite or to pain. Hence, I suppose, comes our slight contempt for men of actionmen, we assume, who don't think. Still, there's no harm in putting a full stop to one's disagreeable thoughts by looking at a mark on the wall.

Indeed, now that I have fixed my eyes upon it, I feel that I have grasped a plank in the sea; I feel a satisfying sense of reality which at once turns the two Archbishops and the Lord High Chancellor to the shadows of shades. Here is something definite, something real. Thus, waking from a midnight dream of horror, one hastily turns on the light and lies quiescent, worshipping the chest of drawers, worshipping solidity, worshipping reality, worshipping the impersonal world which is a proof of some existence other than ours. That is what one wants to be sure of.... Wood is a pleasant thing to think about. It comes from a tree; and trees grow, and we don't know how they grow. For years and years they grow, without paying any attention to us, in meadows, in forests, and by the side of riversall things one likes to think about. The cows swish their tails beneath them on hot afternoons; they paint rivers so green that when a moorhen dives one expects to see its feathers all green when it comes up again. I like to think of the fish balanced against the stream like flags blown out; and of water-beetles slowly raising domes of mud upon the bed of the river. I like to think of the tree itself: first the close dry sensation of being wood; then the grinding of the storm; then the slow, delicious ooze of sap. I like to think of it, too, on winter's nights standing in the empty field with all leaves close-furled, nothing tender exposed to the iron bullets of the moon, a naked mast upon an earth that goes tumbling, tumbling, all night long. The song of birds must sound very loud and strange in June; and how cold the feet of insects must feel upon it, as they make laborious progresses up the creases of the bark, or sun themselves upon the thin green awning of the leaves, and look straight in front of them with diamond-cut red eyes.... One by one the fibres snap beneath the immense cold pressure of the earth, then the last storm comes and, falling, the highest branches drive deep into the ground again. Even so, life isn't done with; there are a million patient, watchful lives still for a tree, all over the world, in bedrooms, in ships, on the pavement, lining rooms, where men and women sit after tea, smoking cigarettes. It is full of peaceful thoughts, happy thoughts, this tree. I should like to take each one separatelybut something is getting in the way.... Where was I? What has it all been about? A tree? A river? The Downs? Whitaker's Almanack? The fields of asphodel? I can't remember a thing. Everything's moving, falling, slipping, vanishing.... There is a vast upheaval of matter. Someone is standing over me and saying

"I'm going out to buy a newspaper."

"Yes?"

"Though it's no good buying newspapers.... Nothing ever happens. Curse this war; God damn this war!... All the same, I don't see why we should have a snail on our wall."

Ah, the mark on the wall! It was a snail.

# The String Quartet

WELL, HERE WE are, and if you cast your eye over the room you will see that Tubes and trams and omnibuses, private carriages not a few, even, I venture to believe, landaus with bays in them, have been busy at it, weaving threads from one end of London to the other. Yet I begin to have my doubts

If indeed it's true, as they're saying, that Regent Street is up, and the Treaty signed, and the weather not cold for the time of year, and even at that rent not a flat to be had, and the worst of influenza its after effects; if I bethink me of having forgotten to write about the leak in the larder, and left my glove in the train; if the ties of blood require me, leaning forward, to accept cordially the hand which is perhaps offered hesitatingly

"Seven years since we met!"

"The last time in Venice."

"And where are you living now?"

"Well, the late afternoon suits me the best, though, if it weren't asking too much"

"But I knew you at once!"

"Still, the war made a break"

If the mind's shot through by such little arrows, andfor human society compels itno sooner is one launched than another presses forward; if this engenders heat and in addition they've turned on the electric light; if saying one thing does, in so many cases, leave behind it a need to improve and revise, stirring besides regrets, pleasures, vanities, and desiresif it's all the facts I mean, and the hats, the fur boas, the gentlemen's swallow-tail coats, and pearl tie-pins that come to the surfacewhat chance is there?

Of what? It becomes every minute more difficult to say why, in spite of everything, I sit here believing I can't now say what, or even remember the last time it happened.

"Did you see the procession?"

"The King looked cold."

"No, no, no. But what was it?"

"She's bought a house at Malmesbury."

"How lucky to find one!"

On the contrary, it seems to me pretty sure that she, whoever she may be, is damned, since it's all a matter of flats and hats and sea gulls, or so it seems to be for a hundred people sitting here well dressed, walled in, furred, replete. Not that I can boast, since I too sit passive on a gilt chair, only turning the earth above a buried memory, as we all do, for there are signs, if I'm not mistaken, that we're all recalling something, furtively seeking something. Why fidget? Why so anxious about the sit of cloaks; and gloveswhether to button or unbutton? Then watch that elderly face against the dark canvas, a moment ago urbane and flushed; now taciturn and sad, as if in shadow. Was it the sound of the second violin tuning in the ante-room? Here they come; four black figures, carrying instruments, and seat themselves facing the white squares under the downpour of light; rest the tips of their bows on the music stand; with a simultaneous movement lift them; lightly poise them, and, looking across at the player opposite, the first violin counts one, two, three

Flourish, spring, burgeon, burst! The pear tree on the top of the mountain. Fountains jet; drops descend. But the waters of the Rhone flow swift and deep, race under the arches, and sweep the trailing water leaves, washing shadows over the silver fish, the spotted fish rushed down by the swift waters, now swept into an eddy whereit's difficult thisconglomeration of fish all in a pool; leaping, splashing, scraping sharp fins; and such a boil of current that the yellow pebbles are churned round and round, round and roundfree now, rushing downwards, or even somehow ascending in exquisite spirals into the air; curled like thin shavings from under a plane, up and up....How lovely goodness is in those who, stepping lightly, go smiling through the world! Also in jolly old fishwives, squatted under arches, obscene old women, how deeply they laugh and shake and rollick, when they walk, from side to side, hum, hah!

"That's an early Mozart, of course"

"But the tune, like all his tunes, makes one despairI mean hope. What do I mean? That's the worst of music! I want to dance, laugh, eat pink cakes, yellow cakes, drink thin, sharp wine. Or an indecent story, nowI could relish that. The older one grows the more one likes indecency. Hah, hah! I'm laughing. What at? You said nothing, nor did the old gentleman opposite....But supposesupposeHush!"

The melancholy river bears us on. When the moon comes through the trailing willow boughs, I see your face, I hear your voice and the bird singing as we pass the osier bed. What are you whispering? Sorrow, sorrow. Joy, joy. Woven together, like reeds in moonlight. Woven together, inextricably commingled, bound in pain and strewn in sorrowcrash!

The boat sinks. Rising, the figures ascend, but now leaf thin, tapering to a dusky wraith, which, fiery tipped, draws its twofold passion from my heart. For me it sings, unseals my sorrow, thaws compassion, floods with love the sunless world, nor, ceasing, abates its tenderness but deftly, subtly, weaves in and out until in this pattern, this consummation, the cleft ones unify; soar, sob, sink to rest, sorrow and joy.

Why then grieve? Ask what? Remain unsatisfied? I say all's been settled; yes; laid to rest under a coverlet of rose leaves, falling. Falling. Ah, but they cease. One rose leaf, falling from an enormous height, like a little parachute dropped from an invisible balloon, turns, flutters waveringly. It won't reach us.

"No, no. I noticed nothing. That's the worst of musicthese silly dreams. The second violin was late, you say?"

"There's old Mrs. Munro, feeling her way outblinder each year, poor womanon this slippery floor."

Eyeless old age, grey-headed Sphinx....There she stands on the pavement, beckoning, so sternly, the red omnibus.

"How lovely! How well they play! Howhowhow!"

The tongue is but a clapper. Simplicity itself. The feathers in the hat next me are bright and pleasing as a child's rattle. The leaf on the plane-tree flashes green through the chink in the curtain. Very strange, very exciting.

"Howhowhow!" Hush!

These are the lovers on the grass.

"If, madam, you will take my hand"

"Sir, I would trust you with my heart. Moreover, we have left our bodies in the banqueting hall. Those on the turf are the shadows of our souls."

"Then these are the embraces of our souls." The lemons nod assent. The swan pushes from the bank and floats dreaming into midstream.

"But to return. He followed me down the corridor, and, as we turned the corner, trod on the lace of my petticoat. What could I do but cry 'Ah!' and stop to finger it? At which he drew his sword, made passes as if he were stabbing something to death, and cried, 'Mad! Mad! Mad!' Whereupon I screamed, and the Prince, who was writing in the large vellum book in the oriel window, came out in his velvet skull-cap and furred slippers, snatched a rapier from the wallthe King of Spain's gift, you knowon which I escaped, flinging on this cloak to hide the ravages to my skirtto hide...But listen! The horns!"

The gentleman replies so fast to the lady, and she runs up the scale with such witty exchange of compliment now culminating in a sob of passion, that the words are indistinguishable though the meaning is plain enoughlove, laughter, flight, pursuit, celestial blissall floated out on the gayest ripple of tender endearmentuntil the sound of the silver horns, at first far distant, gradually sounds more and more distinctly, as if seneschals were saluting the dawn or proclaiming ominously the escape of the lovers....The green garden, moonlit pool, lemons, lovers, and fish are all dissolved in the opal sky, across which, as the horns are joined by trumpets and supported by clarions there rise white arches firmly planted on marble pillars....Tramp and trumpeting. Clang and clangour. Firm establishment. Fast foundations. March of myriads. Confusion and chaos trod to earth. But this city to which we travel has neither stone nor marble; hangs enduring; stands unshakable; nor does a face, nor does a flag greet or welcome. Leave then to perish your hope; droop in the desert my joy; naked advance. Bare are the pillars; auspicious to none; casting no shade; resplendent; severe. Back then I fall, eager no more, desiring only to go, find the street, mark the buildings, greet the applewoman, say to the maid who opens the door: A starry night.

"Good night, good night. You go this way?"

"Alas. I go that."